The Men
from P.I.G. and
R.O.B.O.T.

The Men from P.I.G. and R.O.B.O.T.

by Harry Harrison

Atheneum　　**1979**　　*New York*

Library of Congress Cataloging in Publication Data

Harrison, Harry.
The men from P.I.G. and R.O.B.O.T.

SUMMARY: Humorous accounts of specially trained and bred
pigs and of the Robot Obtrusion Batallion give eleven
thousand new space policemen insight into possible
assignments.
[1. Science fiction]   I. Title
PZ7.H249Me   [Fic.]   77-22875
ISBN 0-689-30634-2

Published simultaneously in Canada by
McClelland & Stewart, Ltd.
Manufactured in the United States of America by
The Book Press, Brattleboro, Vermont
First Printing January 1978
Second Printing August 1978
Third Printing March 1979

Contents

The Graduates   9

The Man From P.I.G.   11

The Man From R.O.B.O.T.   68

Contents

The Men
from P.I.G. and
R.O.B.O.T.

The Graduates

---

*There were over eleven thousand of them drawn up in ramrod
ranks in the great hall. Firm of chin, wide of shoulder, keen of
eye, the finest of the finest, the best young men drawn from all
the planets of man. And now, after years of effort, they were
graduating. In a few moments they would no longer be student
cadets—but full-fledged members of the Patrol.*

The Patrol! *The warriors and policemen of space, the mighty
men who stood between the civilized planets and the chaos of the
galaxy. No men stronger, none more envied.*

*The Commanding Officer looked out at their faces, smiling
despite his normal stern manner, happy to welcome them to the
ranks. When he spoke there was absolute silence.*

*"Patrolmen, I welcome you. When you leave here you will no
longer be cadets—but men of the Patrol. You will wear the uniform
proudly and will be of credit to your calling. Some of you will man
the giant space battleships that guard against alien invasions.
Others will have the lonely vigil of the scoutships. Those of you
who are technically minded have already shown interest in sub-
scape communication, radar installations, engineering. The
Patrol needs every man, needs every talent, and all are equal who
wear the uniform.*

*"Therefore I ask those of you who are of a particularly
adventurous bent of mind to consider the Special Assignments.*

9

You have heard very little about these because they are one of the best kept Patrol secrets. Now the time has come to hear more. As a perfect example of the operations of Special Assignments I will tell you about the troubles on a planet called Trowbri, and just how those problems were resolved."

The Man from P.I.G.

1

"This is the end of our troubles, Governor, it sure is!" the farmer said. The rustic next to him nodded agreement and was moved enough by the thought to lift the hat from his head, shout *Yipppee* once, then clamp it back on.

"Now, I can't positively promise anything," Governor Haydin said; but there was more than a hint of eagerness in his words, and he twirled his moustache with extraordinary exuberance. "Don't know any more about this than you do. We radioed for help, and the Patrol said they'd do something . . ."

"And now a starcruiser is in orbit up there and her tender is on the way down," the farmer broke in, finishing the Governor's sentence. "Sounds good enough for me. Help is on the way!"

The heavens boomed an answer to his words, and a spike of brilliant flame burned through the low-lying clouds above the field as the stubby form of the tender came into view. The crowd along the edge—almost the entire population of Trowbri City—burst into a ragged cheer. They restrained themselves as the ship rode its fiery exhaust down to the muddy field, settling in a cloud of steam; but as soon as the jets flicked off, they surged forward to surround it.

"What's in there, Governor," someone asked, "a company of space commandos or suchlike?"

"The message didn't say—just asked for a landing clearance."

There was a hushed silence as the gangway ground out of its slot below the port and the end clattered down into the mud. The outer hatch swung open with the shrill whine of an electric motor, and a man stepped into the opening and looked down at the crowd.

"Hi," he said. Then he turned and waved inside. "C'mon out, you-all," he shouted, and he put his fingers to his lips and whistled shrilly.

His words evoked a chorus of high pitched cries and squeals from inside the tender. Then out of the port and down the gangway swept a thundering wave of animals. Their backs—pink, black-and-white, and grey—bobbed up and down, and their hooves beat out a rumble of sound on the perforated metal.

"Pigs!" the Governor shouted, his angry voice rising over the chorus of porcine squeals. "Is there nothing but pigs aboard this ship?"

"There's me, sir," the man said, stopping in front of the Governor. "Wurber's my name, Bron Wurber, and these here are my animals. I'm mighty glad to meet you."

Governor Haydin's eyes burned a track up from the ground, slowly consuming every inch of the tall man who stood before him—taking in the high rubber boots; the coarse material of the crumpled trousers; the heavy, stained folds of the once-red jacket; the wide, smiling face and clear blue eyes of the pig farmer. The Governor winced when he saw the bits of straw in the man's hair. He completely ignored Wurber's outstretched hand.

"What are you doing here?" Haydin demanded.

"Come to homestead. Figure to open me a pig ranch. It'll be the only pig ranch for more'n fifty light-years in any direction—and not meanin' to boast, that's sayin' a lot." He wiped his right hand on his jacket, then slowly extended it again. "Name's Wurber; most folk call me Bron because that's my first name. I'm afraid I didn't catch yours?"

"Haydin," the Governor said, reluctantly extending his hand. "I'm the Governor here." He looked down abstractedly at the rounded, squealing forms that milled about them in a churning circle.

"Why, I'm that pleased to meet you, Governor. It's sure a big job you got here," Bron said, happily pumping the other's hand up and down.

The rest of the spectators were already leaving; and when one of the pigs—a great, rounded sow—came too close to them, a man turned and lashed out an ironshod boot. Her shrill screams sliced the air like a buzz saw run wild as she fled.

"Here, none of that," Bron shouted over the backs of his charges. The angry man just shook his fist backward and went away with the rest of the crowd.

"Clear the area," an amplified voice bellowed from the tender. "Blast-off in one minute. Repeat, sixty seconds to blast-off."

Bron whistled again and pointed to a grove of trees at the edge of the field. The pigs squealed in answer and

13

began moving in that direction. The trucks and cars were pulling out, and when the churning herd—with Bron and the Governor at its centre—reached the edge of the field, only the Governor's car was left. Bron started to say something, but his words were drowned out by the tender's rockets and the deafening squealing and grunting of fright that followed it. When it died away, he spoke again.

"If you're drivin' into the city, sir, I wonder if you'd let me drive along with you. I have to file my land claims and all that kind of paper work."

"You wouldn't want to do that," the Governor said, groping around for an excuse to get rid of the rustic clod. "This herd is valuable property; you wouldn't want to leave all these pigs here alone."

"Do you mean there're criminals and *thieves* in your town?"

"I didn't say that," Haydin snapped. "The people here are as decent and law-abiding as any you can find. It's just that, well, we're a little short of meat animals and the sight of all that fresh pork on the hoof . . ."

"Why, that notion is plumb criminal, Governor. This is the finest breedin' stock that money can buy, and none of them are for slaughterin'. Do you realize that every critter here will eventually be the ancestor of entire herds of . . ."

"Just spare me the lecture on animal husbandry. I'm needed in the city."

"Can't keep the good folks waitin'," Bron said with a wide and simple smile. "I'll drive in with you and make my own way back. I'm sure these swine will be safe enough here. They can root around in this patch of woods and take care of themselves for a bit."

"Well it's your funeral—or maybe theirs," Haydin mumbled, getting into the electric car and slamming the door behind him. He looked up with a sudden thought as Bron climbed in the other side. "Say—where's your luggage? Did you forget it in the tender?"

"Now, that's shore nice of you to worry about me like that." Bron pointed out at the herd, which had separated a bit now that the swine were rooting happily in the forest humus. A large boar had two long cases strapped to his back, and a smaller pig nearby had a battered suitcase tied on at a precarious angle.

"People don't appreciate how all-around valuable pigs are. On Earth they been beasts of burden for umpteen thousands of years, yessir. Why there's nothing as all-around as a pig. The old Egyptians used them for plantin' seeds. You know, their bitty little sharp hooves just trod those seeds down to the right depth in the soft soil."

Governor Haydin jammed the rheostat full on and drove numbly into town with a bucolic discourse on swinology echoing about his head.

2

"Is that your municipal buildin'?" Bron asked. "It shore is pretty."

The Governor braked the electric car to a sliding stop in front of the structure, and the dust from the unpaved street rose in a swirling cloud around them. He frowned suspiciously at Bron.

"You're in no position to make fun," he snapped. "It so happens that this was one of the first buildings we put up, and it serves its function even if it is . . . well . . . getting old."

It was more than just old, he realized, really looking at it for the first time in years. It was absolutely *hairy*. The outer walls were made of panels of compressed, shredded wood. These had been plastic-dipped for strength, then cured. But the curing hadn't always taken in the old days. The surface plastic had peeled away, and brown wood shavings were curling out from the surface.

"I ain't making fun of yore buildin'," Bron said, climbing out of the car. "I seen a lot worse on other frontier planets—fallin' down and leanin', that kind of thing. You folks put up a good strong buildin' here. Lasted a lot of years and it's gonna last a lot more." He patted the wall, in a friendly manner, then looked at the palm of his hand. "Though it could sure do with a bit of a shave or a haircut."

Governor Haydin stamped into the entrance, growling to himself, and Bron followed, smiling with simple contentment. The hallway cut through the entire building—he could see the rear entrance at the far end—and doors opened off it on both sides. The Governor pushed through a door marked NO ENTRANCE, and Bron followed close behind him.

"Not in here, you fool," Governor Haydin complained loudly. "This is my private office. The next door, that's the one you want."

"Now, I'm right sorry about that," Bron said, backing out under the firm pressure of the hand on his chest. The room was a sparsely furnished office with living quarters visible through the open door on the far wall. The only thing of real interest was the girl who was slumped in the armchair. She had coppery red hair, was slim, and appeared to be young. He could tell nothing more about her because she had her face buried in a handkerchief and seemed to be crying. The door closed in his face.

The next entrance led him into a larger office divided across the middle by a waist-high counter. He rested his weight on the unpainted wood and read the doodled inscriptions with some interest until a door opened on the other side and a girl entered. She was young and slim and had coppery red hair and even redder eyes. She was undoubtedly the girl he had seen in the Governor's office.

"I'm real sorry to see you cryin', Miss," he said. "Is there anything I can do to help?"

"I am *not* crying," she said firmly, then sniffed. "It's just . . . an allergy, that's all it is."

"You should have a doc give you some shots . . ."

"If you will kindly state your business, I'm rather busy today."

"Now, I don't want to bother you none, what with the allergy and being busy. If there is anyone else I can see?"

"No one. I—and those banks of computers—are the entire governmental staff. What is it you want?"

"I want to file a homestead claim, and my name is Bron Wurber."

She took his extended hand briefly, then dropped it as though it were red hot and grabbed up a stack of papers.

"I'm Lea Davies. Fill out all these forms and do not leave any blanks. If you have any questions, ask me before you proceed. You *can* write, can't you?" she asked, noting his grim frown of concentration as he examined the papers.

"I write a very fair hand, ma'am, so don't you worry none." He took a well-chewed pencil stump from his shirt pocket, added a few more indentations, then went to work.

When he had finished she checked the papers, made some corrections, then handed him a sheaf of maps. "These show all the nearer sites that are open for home-steading; they're marked in red. The land that will suit you best depends, of course, on the kind of crops you intend to raise."

"Pigs," he said, smiling enthusiastically, though there was no smile in return. "I'll just wander around and look at these parcels, then come back and tell you when I find the right one. My thanks, Miss Davies."

Bron folded the papers into a thick wad, which he stuffed into his hip pocket as he left. In order to reach his herd, waiting near the spaceport, he had to walk back through the centre of Trowbri City, which was a city in name only. Clouds of dust spurted up as he stumped along its single street, clumsy in his heavy boots. All of the buildings had a temporary-permanent look. They had been built quickly but never replaced, since more new structures had been in constant demand for the growing town. Pre-fabricated buildings and pressurized fabric huts were interspersed with wood-frame structures and rammed-earth buildings. There were a lot of these—just clayey soil dumped between wooden forms and pounded down hard. When the forms were removed, the walls were painted with plastic so that they would not dissolve in the rain. In spite of this, many of them had a squat, rounded look as they sank slowly back into the ground from whence they had sprung. Bron passed small stores and a garage. The factories were on the outskirts of the town, and beyond them the farms. A barber shop, advertised by the universal symbol of a red-and-white-striped pole, was ahead, and a small group of men were leaning against its wall to hold it up.

"Hey, pig-boy," one of them said loudly as he passed, "I'll trade you a hot bath for a couple of pork chops." The rest of the loafers laughed loudly at what they apparently considered wit.

Bron stopped and turned. "My," he said, "this town must shore be boomin' if it can afford to support so many young fellers who don't have jobs."

There were angry mumbles at this, and their self-appointed spokesman stepped forward and shouted, "You think you're smart or something?"

Bron didn't answer. He just smiled coldly and smacked his closed fist into the palm of his hand. It made a loud, splatting sound, and it was obviously a large and hard fist. The men leaned back against the wall and began to talk among themselves, ignoring him.

"He's a trouble-maker, boys, and you ought to teach him a lesson," a voice called from inside the barber shop. Bron stepped up and looked through the open door. The man who had kicked one of his pigs at the spaceport was sitting in the chair with the robot barber buzzing happily behind him.

"Now, you shouldn't say that, friend, seein' as how you don't know anythin' really about me."

"No, and I don't intend to," the man said angrily. "You can just take your pigs and . . ."

Bron, still smiling, leaned over and pressed the HOT TOWEL button, and a steaming towel muffled the rest of the man's words. The robot snipped off a strip of towelling before its emergency light flashed on and it jerked to a stop, humming loudly. Bron left, and no one barred his way.

"Not a very friendly town," he said to himself. "But why shouldn't it be?" A sign said EAT, and he turned into a small cafe.

"All out of steak," the counterman said.

"Coffee, just coffee is what I want," Bron told him, sitting down on one of the stools. "Nice town you got here," he said when the coffee arrived.

The man mumbled something inaudible and took Bron's money. Bron tried again.

"I mean you got real good farmin' land here, and plenty of minerals and mines. The Space Settlement Commission is staking me to my homestead. Must have staked everyone else here. It's a nice planet."

"Mister," the counterman said, "I don't talk to you, so you don't talk to me. Okay?" He turned away without waiting for an answer and began polishing the dials on the automatic chef.

"Friendly," Bron said as he walked back down the road. "They have everything here they could possibly need—yet no one seems very happy about it. And that girl *was* crying. What is wrong with this planet?" Hands

20

in pockets, whistling lightly through his teeth, he strolled along, looking about him as he went. It was not too far to the spaceport, which was situated a little beyond the town—just a cleared area and a control tower.

As he came near the grove where he had left his animals, he heard a shrill, angry squealing. He quickened his pace, then broke into a ground-consuming run as other squeals joined the first. Some of the pigs were still rooting unconcernedly, but most of them were gathered about a tall tree that was entwined with creepers and studded with short branches. A boar reared his head out of the milling herd and slashed at the tree, peeling away a yard-long strip of bark. From high in the tree a hoarse voice called for help.

Bron whistled instructions, pulled on tails, and pushed on fat flanks and finally got the pigs moving about again. As soon as they began rooting and stripping the berries from the bushes, he called up into the tree.

"Whoever's there can come down now. It's safe."

The tree shook and a patter of bits of bark fell, and a tall, skinny man climbed down slowly into view. He stopped above Bron's head, holding tightly to the trunk. His trousers were torn and the heel was gone from one boot.

"Who are you?" Bron asked.

"Are these your beasts?" the man said angrily. "They ought to all be shot. They attacked me, viciously; would have killed me if I hadn't got to this tree . . ."

"Who are you?" Bron repeated.

". . . vicious and uncontrolled. If you don't take care of them, I will. We have laws here on Trowbri . . ."

"If you don't shut up and tell me who you are, Mister, you can just stay in that tree until you rot," Bron said quietly. He pointed to the large boar, who was lying down about ten feet from the tree and glaring at it out of tiny, red eyes. "I don't have to do anything and these pigs will take care of you all by themselves. It's in their blood. Peccaries in Mexico will tree a man and then take turns standing guard below until he dies or falls out. These animals here don't attack no one without reason. I say the reason is you came by and tried to grab up one of the sucklings because you had a sudden yearning for fresh pork. Who are you?"

"You calling me a liar?" the man shouted.

"Yes. Who are you?"

The boar came over and butted against the tree and made a deep grumbling noise. The man clutched the tree with both arms, and all the air went out of him.

"I'm—Reymon—the radio operator here. I was in the tower landing the tender. When it left I grabbed my cycle and started back to town. I saw these pigs here and I stopped, just to have a look, and that's when I was attacked. Without reason . . ."

"Shore, shore," Bron said. He dug his toe into the boar's side and scraped it up and down on the heavy ribs. The boar flapped his ears and rumbled a happy grunt. "You like it up in that tree, Mr. Reymon?"

"All right, then, I bent down to touch one of your filthy animals—don't ask me why. Then I was attacked."

"That sounds more like it, and I'm not gonna bother you with foolish questions as to why you had a sudden urge to pet a filthy pig. You can come down now and get on your red wagon and get moving."

The boar flicked his twist of a tail, then vanished into the undergrowth. Reymon shakily dropped to the ground and brushed off his clothes. He was a darkly handsome man whose features were spoiled by the angry tightness of his mouth.

"You'll hear more about this," he said over his shoulder as he stumbled away.

"I doubt it," Bron told him. He went to the road and waited until the electrobike whizzed by in the direction of the city. Only then did he go back and whistle his flock together.

3

A TINY metallic clanging sounded in Bron's ear, growing louder and louder when he ignored it. Yawning, he reached up and detached the ear-ring alarm from the lobe of his ear, switched it off with his fingernail, and dropped it into his belt pouch. The night air was cool on his hand as he rubbed the sleep from his eyes, and above him the strange constellations of stars shone crisply in the clear air. Dawn was still some hours away and the forest was dark and silent, with only an occasional wheeze or a muffled grunt sounding from a sleeping pig.

Otherwise completely dressed, Bron unsealed the sleeping bag and pulled on his boots, which he had left carefully up-ended to keep them dry. He leaned against

Queeny to do this. The 800-pound sow, a dim and mountainous shape in the darkness, lifted her head and grunted an interrogation. Bron bent over and lifted the flap of her ear so he could whisper into it.

"I'm going away, but I'll be back by dawn. I'm taking Jasmine with me. You look after things."

Queeny grunted a very human sound of agreement and lay back down. Bron whistled softly, and there was a rustle of sharp hooves as little Jasmine trotted up. "Follow me," he told her. She came to heel and walked behind him away from the camp, both of them now silent as shadows.

It was a moonless night, and Trowbri City was lightless and asleep. No one was aware of the shadows that moved through the town and slipped behind the municipal building. No one heard when a window slid soundlessly open and the shadows vanished from sight.

Governor Haydin sat up suddenly as the lights came on in his bedroom. The first thing he saw was a small pink pig sitting on the rug by his bed. It turned its head to look him directly in the eye—then winked. It had lovely, long white eyelashes.

"Sorry to disturb you at this hour," Bron said from the window, as he made sure the curtains were completely drawn, "but I didn't want anyone to see us meeting."

"Get out of here, you insane swineherd, before I throw you out!" Haydin bellowed.

"Not so loud sir," Bron cautioned. "You may be overheard. Here is my identification." He held out a plastic rectangle.

"I know who you are, so what difference . . ."

"Not this identification. You did ask the Patrol for aid on this planet, didn't you?"

"What do you know about that?" The Governor's eyes widened at the thought. "You mean to say you have something to do with them?"

"My identification," Bron said, snapping to attention and handing over the card.

Governor Haydin grabbed it with both hands. "P.I.G." he read. "What's that?" Then he answered his own question in a hoarse voice as he read the next line.

"*Porcine Interstellar Guard!* Is this some kind of joke?"

"Not at all, Governor. The Guard has only been recently organized and activated. Knowledge of its activities has heretofore been confined to command levels, where its operational configurations are top secret."

"All of a sudden you don't sound like a pig farmer any more."

"I am a pig farmer, Governor. But I have a degree in animal husbandry, a doctorate in galactic politics, and a black belt in judo. The pig farmer is used for field cover."

"Then—*you're* the answer to my distress message to the Patrol?"

"That's correct. I can't give you any classified details, but you must surely know how thin the Patrol is spread these days—and will be for years to come. When a new planet is opened up it extends Earth's sphere of influence in a linear direction—but the volume of space that must be controlled is the *cube* of that distance."

"You wouldn't mind translating that into English, would you?"

"Happily." Bron looked around and spotted a bowl of

fruit on the table. He took out two round red pieces and held them up. "This piece of fruit is a 'sphere of influence.' If Earth is at the centre of the fruit, space ships can fly out in any direction to the skin of the fruit, and all of the fruit inside this sphere must be watched by Earth. All right, let's say that another planet is opened up. The spacer flies in a straight line away from Earth, this far." He held his fingers up to show a distance as long as the diameter of one of the pieces of fruit. "That is a linear distance, in a line; but the Patrol doesn't just patrol in straight lines." He put the second fruit next to the first so that they touched. "The Patrol now has to be responsible for the entire area inside this second fruit, a three-dimensional distance, because spacers do not always follow the same routes, and they go to different destinations. The job is a big one and getting bigger all the time."

"I see what you mean," the Governor said, studying the fruit for a moment, then putting it back into the bowl.

"That's the core of our problem. The Patrol must operate between all the planets, and the volume of space that this comprises is beyond imagining. Some day, it is hoped, there will be enough Patrol vessels to fill this volume so that a cruiser can answer any call for help. But as it stands now, other means of assistance must be found. A number of projects are being instigated, and P.I.G. is one of the first to go operational. You've seen my unit. We can travel by any form of commercial transportation, so we can operate without Patrol assistance. We carry rations, but if need be are self-supporting. We are equipped to handle almost any tactical situation."

Haydin was trying to understand, but it was still all too much for him. "I hear what you're saying. Still . . ." he faltered; ". . . still, all you have is a herd of pigs."

Bron grabbed his temper hard, and his eyes narrowed to slits with the effort. "Would you have felt better if I had landed with a pack of wolves? Would that have given you some sense of security?"

"Well, I do admit that it would look a good deal different. I could see some sense in that."

"Can you? In spite of the fact that a wolf—or wolves— in their natural state will run from a full-grown wild boar without ever considering attacking him? And I have a mutated boar out there that will take on any six wolves and produce six torn wolf skins in about as many minutes. Do you doubt that?"

"It's not a matter of doubt. But you have to admit that there is something . . . I don't know . . . ludicrous, maybe, about a herd of pigs."

"That observation is not exactly original," Bron said in a toneless, arctic voice. "In fact, that is the reason I take the whole herd rather than just boars, and why I do the dumb-farmer bit. People take no notice and it helps my investigation. Which is also why I am seeing you at night like this. I don't want to blow my cover until I have to."

"That's one thing you won't have to worry about. Our problem doesn't involve any of the settlers."

"What exactly *is* your problem? Your message wasn't exactly clear on that point."

Governor Haydin looked uncomfortable. He wriggled a bit, then examined Bron's identification again. "I'll have to check this before I can tell you anything."

"Please do."

There was a fluoroscope on the end table, and Haydin made a thorough job of comparing the normally invisible pattern with the code book he took from his safe. Finally, almost reluctantly, he handed back the card. "It's authentic," he said.

Bron slipped the card back into his pocket. "Now, what is the trouble?" he asked.

Haydin looked at the small pig that was curled up on the rug, snoring happily. "It's ghosts," he said in a barely audible voice.

"And you're the one who laughs at pigs?"

"There's no need to get offensive," the Governor answered hotly. "I know it sounds strange, but there it is. We call them—or the phenomenon—'ghosts' because we don't know anything about it. Whether it's supernatural or not is anyone's guess, but it's sure not physical." He turned to the map on the wall and tapped a yellowish-tan area that stood out from the surrounding green. "Right here, the Ghost Plateau—that's where the trouble is."

"What sort of trouble?"

"It's hard to say—just a feeling mostly. Ever since this planet was settled, going on fifteen years now, people haven't liked to go near the plateau, even though it lies almost directly outside the city. It doesn't feel right up there, somehow. Even the animals stay away. And people have disappeared there and no trace has ever been found of them."

Bron looked at the map, following the yellow gradient outline with his finger. "Hasn't it been explored?" he asked.

28

"Of course, in the first survey. And copters still fly over it, and nothing out of the way is ever seen. But only in daylight. No one has ever flown or driven or walked on the Ghost Plateau during the night and lived to tell about it. Nor has a single body ever been found."

The Governor's voice was heavy with grief; there was no doubt that he meant what he said. "Has anything ever been done about this?" Bron asked.

"Yes. We've learned to stay away. This is not Earth, Mr. Wurber, no matter in how many ways it resembles it. It is an alien planet with alien life on it, and this human settlement is just a pinprick in the planet's hide. Who knows what . . . creatures are out there in the night? We are settlers, not adventurers. We have learned to avoid the plateau, at least at night, and we have never had that kind of trouble anywhere else."

"Then why have you called on the Patrol?"

"Because we made a mistake. The old-timers don't talk much these days about the plateau, and a lot of the newcomers believe that the stories are just . . . stories. Some of us had even begun to doubt our own memories. In any case, a prospecting team wanted to look for some new mine sites, and the only untouched area near the city is on the plateau. In spite of our misgivings the team went out, led by an engineer name of Huw Davies."

"Any relation to your assistant?"

"Her brother."

"That explains her agitation. What happened?"

Haydin's eyes were unfocused as he gazed at a fearful memory. "It was horrible," he said. "We took all precautions, of course—followed them by copter during the day and marked their camp. The copters were rigged with lights, and we stood by all night. They had three radios and all of them were in use, so there could be no communication breakdown. We waited all night and there was no trouble. Then, just before dawn—without any alarm or warning—the radios cut out. We got there within minutes, but it was too late.

"What we found is almost too awful to describe. Everything—their equipment, tents, supplies—was destroyed, crushed and destroyed. There was blood everywhere, spattering the broken trees and the ground—but the men were gone, vanished. There were no tracks of animals or men or machines in the area—nothing. The blood was tested; it was human blood. And the fragments of flesh were . . . human flesh."

"There must have been something," Bron insisted. "Some identifying marks, some clues, perhaps the odour of explosive—or something on your radar, since this plateau is so close."

"We are not stupid men. We have technicians and scientists. There were no clues, no smells, nothing on radar. I repeat, nothing."

"And this is when you decided to call the Patrol."

"Yes. This thing is too big for us to handle."

"You were absolutely correct, Governor. I'll take it from here. In fact, I already have a very good idea what happened."

Haydin was jolted to his feet. "You can't! What is it?"

"I'm afraid it is a little too early to say. I'm going up to the plateau in the morning to look at this place where the massacre happened. Can you give me the map coordinates? And please don't mention my visit to any-one."

"Little chance of that," Haydin said, looking at the little pig. It stood and stretched, then sniffed loudly at the bowl of fruit on the table.

"Jasmine would like a piece," Bron said. "You don't mind, do you?"

"Go ahead, help yourself," the Governor said resignedly, and loud chomping filled the room as he wrote down the coordinates and directions.

4

THEY had to hurry to be clear of the town before dawn. By the time they reached their camp the sky was grey in the east and the animals were up and stirring.

"I think we'll stay here at least another day," Bron said as he cracked open a case of vitamin rations. Queeny, the 800-pound Poland China sow, grunted happily at this announcement and rooted up a wad of leaves and tossed them into the air.

"Good foraging, I don't doubt it, particularly after all that time in the ship. I'm going to take a little trip, Queeny, and I'll be back by dark. You keep an eye on things until then." He raised his voice, "Curly! Moe!"

A crashing in the forest echoed his words, and a moment later two long greyish-black forms tore out of the under-brush—a ton of bone and muscle on the hoof. A three-inch branch was in Curly's way, and he neither swerved nor slowed. There was a sharp *crack*, and he skidded up to Bron with the broken branch draped across his back. Bron threw the branch aside and looked at his shock troops.

They were boars, twins from the same litter, and weighed over 1,000 pounds apiece. An ordinary wild boar will weigh up to 750 pounds and is the fastest, most dangerous, and worst-tempered beast ever known. Curly and Moe were mutants, a third again heavier than their wild ancestors and many times as intelligent. But nothing else had changed; they were still just as fast, dangerous, and bad-tempered. Their ten-inch tusks were capped with stainless steel to prevent them from splitting.

"I want you to stay here with Queeny, Moe, and she'll be in charge."

Moe squealed in anger and tossed his great head. Bron grabbed a handful of hide and thick bristles between Moe's shoulder blades, the boar's favourite itch spot, and twisted and pummelled it. Moe blurbled happily through his nose. Moe was a pig genius, which made him on the human level a sort of retarded moron—except that he wasn't human. He understood simple orders and would obey them within the limits of his capacity.

"Stay and guard, Moe, stay and guard. Watch Queeny; she knows what is best. Guard, don't kill. Plenty of good things to eat here—and candy when I get back. Curly goes with me, and everyone gets candy when we come back." There were happy grunts from all directions, and Queeny pressed her fat side against his leg.

"You're coming too, Jasmine," Bron said. "A good

32

walk will keep you out of trouble. Go get Maisie Mule-Foot; the exercise will do her good too."

Jasmine was his problem child. Though she looked only like a half-grown shoat, she was a full-grown Pitman-Moore miniature—one of a strain of small pigs that had originally been developed for use in laboratories. They had been bred for intelligence, and Jasmine probably had the highest I.Q. ever to have come out of the lab. But there was a handicap: With the intelligence went an instability, an almost human hysteria, as though her mind were balanced on a sharp edge. If she were left with the other pigs she would tease and torture them and cause trouble, so Bron made sure that she was with him if he had to be away from the herd for any length of time.

Maisie was a totally different case: a typical, well-rounded sow—a Mule-Foot, a general-purpose breed. Her intelligence was low—or pig normal—and her fecundity high. Some cruel people might have said she was good only for bacon. But she had a pleasant personality and was a good mother; in fact, she had just weaned her last litter. Bron took her along to give her some relief from her weanling progeny—and also to run some fat off her, since she had grown uncommonly plump during the confined space voyage.

Bron examined his maps and found what appeared to be an old logging road that ran in the direction in which he wanted to go, almost as far as the plateau. He and the pigs could go across country easily enough, but they might save some time by following the road. He set his pocket gyrocompass by lining it up with the arms of the control tower's weather vane, then worked out a heading that would reach the road that led to the Ghost Plateau. He pointed his arm in the correct direction, and Curly put his head down and catapulted into the undergrowth. There was a snapping and crackling as he tore his way through—the perfect pathfinder, who made his own openings where none were available.

It was an easy walk as the grass-covered road wound up through the hills. The logging camp must have been closed down for a long time, because the road was free of wheel ruts. The pigs snuffled in the rich grass, grabbing an occasional bite of something too tempting to resist, although Maisie wheezed complaints about the unaccustomed exertion. There were some trees along the road, but for the most part the land was cleared and planted with crops. Curly stopped, wheeled, and pointed into a thick growth of woods, rumbling a questioning grunt. Jasmine and Maisie stopped next to him, looking in the same direction, heads cocked and listening.

"What is it? What's in there?" Bron asked.

It was nothing dangerous, that was clear, since if there had been a threat Curly would have gone charging to the attack. With their more acute hearing the pigs were listening to something he could not hear, something that interested but did not frighten them.

"Let's go," he said. "There's plenty of walking ahead." He pushed against Curly's side; but he could have accomplished just as much by shoving against a stone wall. Curly, unmoving, scratched with a forehoof and tossed his head in the direction of the trees.

"All right, if you insist. I never argue with boars who weigh over half a ton. Let's go see what's in there." He grabbed a handful of thick bristles and hide, and Curly started off among the trees.

Before they had gone fifty yards, Bron could hear the sound himself—a bird or a small animal of some kind, calling shrilly. But why should this bother the pigs? Then, suddenly, he realized what it was.

"That's a child—crying! Come on, Curly!"

With this encouragement Curly trotted forward, pushing his way through the underbrush so fast that Bron could hardly keep up. They came to a steep, muddy bank with a dark pond below, and the crying was now a loud, unhappy sobbing. A little girl, no more than two years old, was up to her waist in the water, wet and unhappy.

"Hold on; I'll have you out in a second," Bron said, and the sobbing turned to a shrill wailing. Curly stood on the brink of the slippery mud slope, and Bron used his sturdy and immobile ankle to hold on to as he let himself down. The child struggled towards him, and he grabbed her with his free hand and pulled her to safety. She was wet and miserable, but she stopped crying as soon as he had her under his arm.

"Now what shall we do with you?" Bron asked when he was on top again, and this time he heard the answer at the same time as the pigs. The distant, continual ringing of a bell. He started them in the right direction, then walked behind in the path that Curly ploughed through the underbrush.

The woods ended at an open meadow. A red farmhouse was on the hill above, where a woman stood waving a large hand bell. She saw Bron as soon as he had emerged from the trees and ran down to meet him.

"Amy," she cried, "you're all right!" She pulled the child to her, ignoring the mud stains on her white apron.

"Found her back there in the pond, ma'am. Got herself stuck in the mud and couldn't get out. More frightened than anything else, I'd say."

"I don't know how to thank you. I thought she was asleep when I went to milk the cows. She must have wandered out . . ."

"Don't thank me, ma'am, thank my pigs here. They heard her cryin', and I just followed them."

For the first time the woman was aware of the animals.

"What a fine Mule-Foot," she said, admiring Maisie's well-rounded lines. "We used to keep pigs at home, but when we emigrated we just bought the cows for a dairy farm. I'm sorry now. Let me give them some fresh milk— you too. It's the least I can do."

"Thank you kindly, but we have to push on. Lookin' for a homestead site, and I want to get up to the plateau and back before dark."

"Not there!" the woman gasped, clutching the little girl to her. "You can't go up there!"

"Any reason why I shouldn't? Looks like good land on the map."

"You can't that's all . . . there are *things*. We don't talk about them much. Things you can't see. I know they're there. We used to keep some cows in that uphill pasture, on the side towards the Ghost Plateau. You know why we stopped? Their milk was off—less than half of what the other cows were producing. There's something wrong up there, *very* wrong. Go look if you must, but you

36

have to leave before dark. You'll find out what I mean
quick enough."

"Thanks for tellin' me; I do appreciate it. So seein' how
the little girl is all right now, I'll just be movin' on."

Bron whistled the pigs to him, waved good-bye to the
farm wife, and made his way back to the road. The
plateau was getting more interesting all the time. He kept
the pigs moving steadily after this, in spite of Maisie's
heavy breathing and unhappy looks, and within an hour
they had passed the deserted logging camp—abandoned
because of the strange happenings on the plateau?—and
started up among the trees. This was the edge of the
plateau.

They crossed a stream, and Bron let the pigs drink their
fill while he cut himself a stick for the climb. Maisie, over-
heated by her exertions, dropped full length into the water
with a tremendous splash and soaked herself. Jasmine, a
fastidious animal, squealed with rage and rushed away to
roll in the grass and dry herself off where she had been
splashed. Curly, with much chuffing and grunting like a
satisfied locomotive, got his nose under a rotting log that
must have weighed nearly a ton and rolled it over and
happily consumed the varied insect and animal life he
found beneath it. They moved on.

It was not a long climb to the plateau, and once they
were over the edge the ground levelled out into a lightly
forested plain. Bron took another compass reading and
pointed Curly in the right direction. Curly snorted and
raked a furrow in the ground with a forehoof before setting
off, and Jasmine pressed up against Bron's leg and
squealed.

Bron could feel it too, and he had to suppress an involuntary shiver. There was something—how could it be described?—*wrong* about this place. He had no idea why he felt this way, but he did. And the pigs seemed to sense it too. There was something else wrong: there was not a bird in sight, although the hills below had been filled with them. And there did not seem to be any other animals about. The pigs would surely have called his attention to any he might have missed.

Bron fought down the strange sensation and followed Curly's retreating hindquarters, while the two other pigs, still protesting, trotted behind him, staying as close to his legs as possible. It was obvious that they all felt this presentiment of danger, and they were all bothered by it. All except Curly, that is, since any strange emotion or sensation just tripped his boarish temper, so that he ploughed ahead filled with mumbling anger.

When they reached the clearing, there was no doubt that it was the correct one. Branches on all sides were bent and twisted, and small trees had been pulled down, while torn tents and crushed equipment littered the area. Bron picked up a transceiver and saw that the metal case had been pinched and twisted, as though squeezed by some giant hand.

And all the time, as he searched the area, he was aware of the tension and pressure.

"Here, Jasmine," he said, "take a smell of this. I know it's been out in the rain and sun for weeks now, but there may be a trace of something left. Give a sniff."

Jasmine shivered and shook her head *no* and pressed up against his legs; he could feel her body shiver. She was in one of her states and good for nothing until it passed. Bron didn't blame her—he felt a little that way himself. He gave Curly the case to smell, and the boar took an obliging sniff, but his attention wasn't really on it. His little eyes scanned in all directions while he smelled it, and then he sniffed around the clearing, snuffling and snorting to blow the dirt out of his nostrils. Bron thought he was on to something when he began to rip the ground with his tusks, but it was only a succulent root that he had smelled. He chomped at it—then suddenly raised his head and pointed his ears at the woods, the root dangling, forgotten, from his jaws.

"What is it?" Bron asked, because the other two animals were pointing in the same direction, listening intently. Their ears twitched, and there was the sudden sound of something large crashing through the bush.

The suddenness of the attack almost finished Bron. The crashing was still sounding some distance away when the Bounder plunged out of the woods almost on top of him, foot-long yellow claws outstretched. Bron had seen pictures of this species of giant marsupials, native to the planet, but the reality was something else again. It stood on its hind legs, twelve feet high, and even the knowledge that it was not carnivorous and used the claws for digging in the marshes was not encouraging. It also used them against its enemies, and he seemed to be in that category at the moment. The creature sprang out, loomed over him; the claws swung down.

Curly, growling with rage, hit the beast from the side. Even twelve feet of brown-furred marsupial cannot stand up to 1,000 pounds of angry boar, and the big beast went over and back. As he passed, Curly flicked his head with a wicked twist that hooked a tusk into the animal's leg and ripped. With a lightning spin the boar reversed direction and returned to the attack.

The Bounder was not having any more. Shrieking with pain and fear, it kept on going in the opposite direction just as its mate—the one that had been blundering through the woods—appeared in the clearing. Curly spun again, reversing within one body length, and charged. The Bounder—this one, because of its size, must have been the male—appraised the situation instantly and did not like it. Its mate was fleeing in pain—and telling everybody about it loudly—and without a doubt this underslung, hurtling mass of evil-looking creature must be to blame. Without slowing, the Bounder kept going and vanished among the trees on the opposite side.

Through the entire affair Jasmine had rushed about, accomplishing very little but obviously on the verge of a nervous breakdown. Maisie, never one for quick reaction, just stood and flapped her ears and grunted in amazement.

As Bron reached into his pocket for a pill to quiet Jasmine down, a long, green snake slithered out of the woods almost at his feet.

He stopped, frozen, with his hand half-way to his pocket, because he knew he was looking at death. This was the Angelmaker, the most poisonous serpent on Trowbri, more deadly than anything Mother Earth had ever produced. It had the meat-hungry appetite of a constrictor—because it was a constrictor in its eating habits— but it also had fangs and well-filled venom sacs. And it

was agitated, weaving back and forth and preparing to
strike.

It was obvious that portly, pink Maisie, sow and
mother, did not have the reflexes or the temperament to
deal with attacking marsupials—but a snake was something else altogether. She squealed and jumped forward,
moving her weight with ponderous agility.

The Angelmaker saw the appealing mass of quivering
flesh and struck, instantly darting its head back and
striking again. Maisie, snorting with the effort to turn her
head and look back over her shoulder, squealed again and
backed towards the poised snake. It hissed loudly and
struck another time, perhaps wondering in some dim
corner of its vestigial brain why this appealing dinner did
not drop down so he could eat it. If the Angelmaker had
known a bit more about pigs, it might have acted differ-
ently. Instead it struck again, and by now most of its
venom was gone.

While the Mule-Foot is not a lardy type, it is a sturdy
breed, and the females do run to fat. Maisie was plumper
than most. Her hindquarters—what some crude carnivorous types might call her hams—were coated with heavy
fat. And there is no blood circulation through fat. The
venom had been deposited in the fat, where it could not
reach the blood stream and could do no injury. Eventually
it would be neutralized by her body chemistry and
disposed of. Right now Maisie was turning the tables. The
Angelmaker struck again—listlessly, because its venom
was gone. Maisie heaved her bulk about and chopped
down with her hooves—strong, sharp-edged weapons.
While snakes may like to kill pigs, pigs also greatly enjoy

eating snakes. Squealing and bouncing heavily, Maisie landed on the snake's spine and neatly amputated its head. The body still writhed and she attacked again, chopping with her hooves until the snake had been cut into a number of now motionless segments. Only then did she stop attacking and begin to mumble happily to herself while she ate them. It was a big snake, and she allowed Curly and Jasmine to help her with it. Bron waited for them to finish before moving out, because the feast was calming them down. Only when the last chunk had vanished did he turn and start back for the camp. He kept looking back over his shoulder and found that it was a great relief—for all of them—to start down the slope away from the Ghost Plateau.

5

WHEN they reached the rest of the herd, there were grunts of greeting. The most intelligent beasts remembered the promised candy and crowded around waiting for it.

Bron opened a case of the mineral-and-vitamin-reinforced delicacy. While distributing it, he heard the buzz of his phone—very dimly, because he had yet to unpack it from its carrying case.

When he had filled out all the homesteading forms he had of course put down his phone number, since this was as much a part of him as was his name. Everyone was given a phone number at birth, and it was his for life. With the computer-controlled circuits anyone, anywhere on a planet, could be reached by the dialling of a single number. But who could be calling him here? As far as he knew, only Lea Davies had his number. He pulled out the compact phone—no bigger than his hand, including its lifetime atomic battery—and flipped up the small screen. This activated the phone, and static rustled from the speaker while a coloured image appeared on the screen.

"Now, I was just thinkin' 'bout you, Miss Davies," he said. "Ain't that a coincidence."

"Very," she said, barely moving her lips when she spoke, as though groping for words. She was a pretty girl, but looking too haggard now. Her brother's death had hit her hard. "I must see you . . . Mr. Wurber. As soon as possible."

"Now, that's right friendly, Miss Lea; I'm lookin' forward to that."

"I need your help, but we musn't be seen talking together. Can you come as soon as it's dark, alone, to the rear entrance of the municipal building? I'll meet you there."

"I'll be there—you can count on me," he said, and he rung off.

What was this about? Did the girl know something no one else knew? It was possible. But why him? Unless the Governor had told her about P.I.G.—which was very possible, since she was his only assistant. And on top of that she was very attractive, when she wasn't crying. As soon as he had fed the herd, he broke out some clean clothes and his razor.

Bron left at dusk, and Queeny lifted her head to watch him go. She would be in charge until he came back—the

43

rest of the pigs knew and expected that—and she had Curly and Moe ready to take care of any trouble that might arise. Curly was sleeping off the day's exertions, whistling placidly through his nose; and next to him little Jasmine was also asleep, even more tired and sedated by a large Miltown. The situation was well in hand.

Approaching the municipal building from its unlighted rear was no problem, since he had been over the same ground just the previous evening. All this running about and missing sleep was getting to him at last, and he choked off a yawn with his fist.

"Miss Lea, are you there?" he called softly, pushing open the unlocked door. The hall beyond was black, and he hesitated.

"Yes, I'm here," her voice called out. "Please come in."

Bron pushed the door wide and stepped through, and a crashing pain struck him across the side of the head, the agony of it for an instant lighting the darkness of his nerves. He tried to say something, but could not speak, though he did manage to raise his arm. Another blow struck his forearm, numbing it so that it dropped away; and the third blow, across the back of his neck, sent him plunging down into a deeper darkness.

"What happened?" the wavering pink blob asked, and with much blinking Bron managed to focus on it and recognized Governor Haydin's worried face.

"You tell me," Bron said hoarsely. He became aware of the pain in his head, and he almost passed out again. Something damp and cool snuffled against his neck, and he worked his hand up to twist Jasmine's ear.

"I thought I told you to get that pig out of here," someone said.

"Leave her be," Bron managed to say, "and tell me what happened." He turned his head, with infinite caution, and saw that he was lying on the couch in the Governor's office. A medical-looking gentleman with a stern face and dangling stethoscope was standing by. There were a number of other people at the doorway.

"We just found you here," the Governor said. "That's all we know. I was working in my office when I heard this screaming, like a girl in terrible pain—something awful. Some of these other men heard it outside in the street, and we all came running. Found you lying in the rear hall—out cold with your head laid open, and this pig standing next to you doing all the screaming. I never knew an animal could sound like that. It wouldn't let anyone near you—kept charging and chomping its teeth in a very threatening manner. Quieted down a bit by the time the doctor came and finally let him get over to you."

Bron thought quickly—or at least as quickly as he could with a power saw trying to take off the back of his head.

"Then you know as much about it as I do," he said. "I came here to see about filing my homesteadin' papers. The front was locked, and I thought maybe I could get in by the back, if anyone was still here. I walked through the back door and somethin' hit me and the next thing I know I was waking up here. Guess I can thank Jasmine here for that. She must have followed me and seen me hit. Must have started squealing, like you heard, and probably chewing on the ankle of whoever hit me. Pigs have very

good teeth. Must have frightened him off, whoever it was."
He groaned; it was easy to do. "Can you give me something for my head, Doctor?" he asked.

"There is a possibility of concussion," the doctor said.

"I'll take my chances on that, Doc; better a little concussion than my head splittin' into two halves this
way."

By the time the doctor had finished and the crowd
dispersed, the pain in his head had subsided to a throbbing
ache, and Bron was fingering the bruise on his arm, which
he had just become aware of. He waited until the Governor
had closed and locked the door before he spoke.

"I didn't tell you the whole story," he said.

"I didn't think you had. Now what is this all about?"

"I was struck by a party or parties unknown—that
much was all true; and if Jasmine had not woken up and
found me missing and gotten all neurotically insecure, I
would probably be dead at this moment. It was a trap,
neatly set up, and I walked right into it."

"What do you mean?"

"I mean that Lea Davies is involved in this. She called
me, arranged to meet me here, and was waiting here when
I arrived."

"Are you trying to say . . ."

"I've said it. Now get the girl in here so we can hear
her side of it."

When the Governor went to the phone, Bron swung his
legs slowly to the floor and wondered what it would feel
like to stand up. It was not nice. He held on to the back
of the couch while the room spun in slow circles and the
floor heaved like a ship at sea. Jasmine leaned against his

leg and moaned in sympathy. After a while, when the moving furniture and rotating building had slowed to a stop, he tried walking and stumbled over to the kitchen.

"May I help you, sir?" the kitchen said when he entered. "Perhaps a little midnight snack is in order?"

"Coffee, just black coffee—lots of it."

"Coming at once, sir. But dieticians do say that coffee can be irritating to an empty stomach. Perhaps a lightly toasted sandwich, or a grilled cutlet . . ."

"Quiet!" His head was beginning to throb again. "I do not like ultramodern robot kitchens with a lot of smart back talk. I like old-fashioned kitchens that flash a light that says *ready*—and that is all they can say."

"Your coffee, sir," the kitchen said, in what was surely a hurt tone. A door snapped open above the counter and a steaming jug emerged. Bron looked around. "And what about a cup—or should I drink it out of the palm of my hand?"

"A cup, *of course*, sir. You did not *specify* that you wanted a cup." There was a muffled clank inside the machine, and a chipped cup rattled down a chute and landed on its side on the table.

Just what I needed, Bron thought. *A temperamental robot kitchen.* Jasmine came in, her little hooves click-clacking on the tiled floor. *I'd better get on the right side of this kitchen or I'll be in trouble with the Governor when he finds out.*

"Now that you mention it, kitchen," he said aloud in the sweetest tones he could summon, "I have heard a great deal about your wonderful cooking. I wonder if you could make me eggs Benedict . . . ?"

"The work of a second, sir," the kitchen said happily,

and only moments later the steaming dish arrived, with folded napkin and knife and fork.

"Wonderful," Bron said, putting the dish down for Jasmine. "The best I ever tasted." Loud smacking and chomping filled the room.

"Indeed you are a fast eater, sir," the kitchen hummed. "Enjoy, enjoy."

Bron took the coffee back to the other room and carefully sat down again on the couch. The Governor looked up from the phone, and he was frowning worriedly. "She's not at home," he said, "or with friends or anywhere that I can determine. A patrol has searched the area, and I sent a net call to all the local phones. No one has seen her—and there is no trace of her anywhere. That can't be possible. I'll try the mine stations."

It took over an hour for Governor Haydin to prove to his own satisfaction that Lea had vanished. The settled portion of Trowbri covered a limited area, and everyone could be reached by phone. No one had seen her or knew where she was. She was gone. Bron had faced this fact long before the Governor would admit it—and he knew what had to be done. He slumped back on the couch, half dozing, with his shoes off and his feet propped on Jasmine's warm flank. The little pig was out like a light, sleeping the sleep of the just.

"She's gone," Haydin said, switching off the last call. "How can it be? She couldn't have had anything to do with your being attacked."

"She could have—if she were forced into it."

"What are you talking about?"

"I'm just guessing, but it makes sense. Suppose her brother were not dead . . ."

"What are you saying?"

"Let me finish. Suppose her brother were alive, but in deadly danger. And she had the chance to save him if she did as ordered—which was to get me here. Give the girl credit: I don't think she knew they meant to kill me. She must have put up a fight—that's why she was taken away too."

"What do you know, Wurber?" Haydin shouted. "Tell me—everything. I'm Governor here and I have a right to know."

"And know you shall—when I have anything more than hunches and guesses to give you. This attack, and the kidnapping, means that someone is unhappy about my presence, which also means that I am getting close. I'm going to speed things up and see if I can catch these 'ghosts' off guard."

"Do you think there is a connection between all this and the Ghost Plateau?"

"I *know* there is. That's why I want word circulated in the morning that I am moving into my homestead to-morrow. Make sure everyone knows where it is."

"Where?"

"On the Ghost Plateau—where else?"

"That's suicide!"

"Not really. I have some guesses as to what happened up there, and some defences—I hope. I also have my team, and they've proved themselves twice today. It will be taking a chance, but I'm going to have to take a chance if we ever hope to see Lea alive again."

49

Haydin clenched his fists on the top of his desk and made up his mind. "I can stop this if I want to—but I won't if you do it my way. Full radio connection, armed guards, the copters standing by . . ."

"No, sir; thank you very much, but I remember what happened to the last bunch that tried it that way."

"Then—I'll go with you myself. I'm responsible for Lea. You'll take me or you won't go."

Bron smiled. "Now, that's a deal, Guv. I could use a helping hand, and maybe a witness. Things are going to get pretty busy on the plateau tonight. But no guns."

"That's suicide."

"Just remember the first expedition, and do it my way. I'm leaving most of my equipment behind. I imagine you can arrange to have it trucked to a warehouse until we get back. I think you'll find I have a good reason for what I'm doing."

BRON managed to squeeze in over ten hours' sleep, because he felt he was going to need it. By noon the truck had come and gone and they were on the way. Governor Haydin was dressed for the occasion, in hunting boots and rough clothes, and he moved right out with them. Not that the pace was so fast; they went at the speed of the slowest piglet, and there was much noisy comment from all sides and grabbing of quick snacks from the roadside. They took the course this time that the original expedition had taken—a winding track that led up to the plateau in easy stages, for the most part running beside a fast river of muddy water. Bron pointed to it.

"Is this the river that runs through the plateau?" he asked.

Haydin nodded. "This is the one; it comes down from that range of mountains back there."

Bron nodded, then ran to rescue a squealing suckling from a crack in the rocks into which it had managed to wedge itself. They moved on.

By sunset they had set up camp—in the glade just next to the one where the previous expedition had met its end.

"Do you think this is a good idea?" Haydin asked.

"The best," Bron told him. "It's the perfect spot for our needs." He eyed the sun, which was close to the horizon. "Let's eat now; I want everything cleared away by dark."

Bron had opened a tremendous tent, but it was sparsely furnished—containing, to be exact, only two folding chairs and a battery-powered light.

"Isn't this a little on the Spartan side?" Haydin asked.

"I see no reason to bring equipment 45 light-years just to have it destroyed. We've obviously set up camp; that's all that's important. The equipment I need is in here." He tapped a small plastic sack that hung from his shoulder. "Now—chow's up."

Their table was an empty ration box that had held the pigs' dinner. A good officer always sees to his troops first, so the animals had been fed. Bron put two self-heating dinners on the box, broke their seals, and handed Haydin a plastic fork. It was almost dark by the time they had finished and Bron leaned out through the open end of the tent and whistled for Curly and Moe. The two boars arrived at full charge and left grooves in the dirt as they skidded to a halt next to him.

"Good boys," he said, scratching their bristly skulls. They grunted happily and rolled their eyes up at him. "They think I'm their mother, you know." He waited placidly while Haydin fought with his expression, his face turning red in the process. "That may sound a little funny, but it's true. They were removed from their litter at birth and I raised them. So I'm 'imprinted' as their parent."

"Their parents were pigs. You don't look very much like a pig to me."

"You've never heard of imprinting. Everyone knows that if a kitten is raised with a litter of pups, the cat goes through life thinking she is another dog. This is more than just association from an early age. There exists a physical process known as imprinting. The way it works is that the first creature an animal is aware of, that it sees when its eyes first open, is recognized as a parent. This usually is a parent—but not always. The kitten thinks the dog is its mother. These two oversized boars think I am their parent, no matter how physically impossible that may appear to you. I made sure of that before I even considered training them. It is the only way I can be absolutely safe around them, since, intelligent as they are, they are still quick-tempered and deadly beasts. It also means that I'm safe as long as they are around. If anyone as much as threatened me he would be disembowelled within the second. I'm telling you this so that you won't try anything foolish. Now, would you kindly hand over that gun you promised not to bring."

Haydin's hand jumped towards his hip pocket—and stopped just as suddenly as both boars turned towards the sudden movement. Moe was salivating with happiness at the head-scratching, and a drop of saliva collected and dropped from the tip of one ten-inch tusk.

"I need it for my own protection . . ." Haydin protested.

"You're better protected without it. Take it out, slowly."

Haydin reached back gingerly and took out a compact energy pistol, then tossed it over to Bron. Bron caught it and hung it on the hook next to the light. "Now empty your pockets," he said. "I want everything metallic dumped on to the box."

"What are you getting at?"

"We'll talk about it later; we don't have time now. Dump."

Haydin looked at the boars and emptied out his pockets, while Bron did the same. They left a collection of coins, keys, knives, and small instruments on the box.

"We can't do anything now about the eyelets in your boots," Bron said, "but I don't think they'll cause much trouble. I took the precaution of wearing elastic-sided boots."

It was dark now, and Bron drove his charges into the woods nearby, spreading them out under the trees a good hundred yards from the clearing. Only Queeny, the intelligent sow, remained behind, dropping down heavily next to Bron's stool.

"I demand an explanation," said Governor Haydin.

"Don't embarrass me, Guv; I'm just working on guesses so far. If nothing has happened by morning, I'll give you an explanation—and my apology. Isn't she a beauty," he added, nodding towards the massive hog at his feet.

"I'm afraid I might use another adjective myself."

"Well, don't say it out loud. Queeny's English is pretty good, and I don't want her feelings hurt.

"Misunderstanding, that's all it is. People call pigs dirty, but that's only because they have been made to live in filth. They're naturally quite clean and fastidious animals. They can be fat. They have a tendency to be sedentary and obese—just like people—so they can put on weight if they have the diet for it. In fact, they are more like human beings than any other animal. They get ulcers like us and heart trouble the same way we do. Like man, they have hardly any hair on their bodies, and even their teeth are similar to ours.

"Their temperaments, too. Centuries ago, an early physiologist by the name of Pavlov, who used to do scientific experiments with dogs, tried to do the same thing with pigs. But as soon as he placed them on the operating table, they would squeal at the top of their lungs and thrash about. He said that they were 'inherently hysterical' and went back to working with dogs. Which shows you, even the best men have a blind spot. The pigs weren't hysterical—they were plain sensible; it was the dogs who were being dim. The pigs reacted just the way a man might if they tried to tie him down for some quick vivisection. . . . What is it, Queeny?"

Bron added this last as Queeny suddenly raised her head, her ears lifted, and grunted.

"Do you hear something?" Bron asked. The pig grunted again, in a rising tone, and climbed to her feet. "Does it sound like engines coming this way?" Queeny nodded her ponderous head in a very human *yes*.

"Get into the woods—back under the trees!" Bron shouted, hauling Haydin to his feet. "Do it fast—or you're dead."

They ran, headlong, and were among the trees when a distant, rising whine could be heard. Haydin started to ask something but was pushed face first into the leaves as a whining, roaring shape floated into the clearing, blackly occulting the stars. It was anything but ghostly—but what was it? A swirl of leaves and debris swept over them, and Haydin felt something pulling at his legs so that they jumped about of their own accord. He tried to ask a question, but his words were drowned out as Bron blew on a plastic whistle and shouted:

"Curly, Moe—*attack!*"

At the same moment, he pulled a stick-like object out of his pack and threw it out into the clearing. It hit, popped, and burst into eye-searing flame—a flare of some kind.

The dark shape was a machine—that was obvious enough: round, black, and noisy, at least ten feet across, floating a foot above the ground, with a number of discs mounted around its edge. One of them swung towards the tent, and there was a series of explosive, popping sounds as the tent seemed to explode and fall to the ground.

There was only a moment to see this before the attacking forms of the boars appeared from the opposite side of the clearing. Their speed was incredible as, heads down and legs churning, they dived at the machine. One of them arrived a fraction of a second before the other and crashed into the machine's flank. There was a metallic clang and the shriek of tortured machinery as it was jarred back, bent, almost tipped over.

The boar on the far side took instant advantage of this, his intelligence as quick as his reflexes, and without slowing hurled himself into the air and over the side and into the open top of the machine. Haydin looked on appalled. The machine was almost on the ground now, as a result of either ruined machinery or the weight of the boar. The angry first animal now climbed the side and also vanished into the interior. Above the roar of the engine could be heard loud crashes and metallic tearing—and high-pitched screaming. Something clattered and tore, and the sound of the engines died away with a descending moan. As the sound lessened, a second machine could be heard approaching.

"Another coming!" Bron shouted, blasting on his whistle as he jumped to his feet. One of the boars popped its head from the ruin of the machine, then leaped out. The other was still noisily at work. The first boar catapulted himself towards the approaching sound and was on the spot when the machine appeared at the edge of the clearing—leaping and attacking, twisting his tusks into the thing. Something tore, and a great black length of material hung down. The machine lurched, and its operator must have seen the ruin of the first one, because it skidded in a tight circle and vanished back in the direction from which it had come.

Bron lit a second flare and tossed it out as the first one flickered. They were two-minute flares, and the entire action—from beginning to end—had taken place in less than that time. He walked over to the ruined machine, and Haydin hurried after him. The boar leaped to the ground and stood there panting, then wiped its tusks on the ground.

"What is it?" Haydin asked.

"A hovercraft," Bron said. "They aren't seen very much these days—but they do have their uses. They can move over any kind of open country or water, and they don't leave tracks. But they can't go over or through forest."

"I've never heard of anything like that."

"You wouldn't have. Since beamed power and energy cells came into general use, better means of transportation have been developed. But at one time they used to build hovercraft as large as houses. They are sort of a cross between ground and air transport. They float in the air, but depend upon the ground for support, since they float on a column of air being blown down out of the bottom."

"You knew this thing was coming—that's why you had us hide in the woods?"

"I suspected this. And for very good reasons, I suspected *them*." He pointed inside the wrecked hovercraft, and Haydin recoiled in shock.

"I tend to forget—I guess everyone does," the Governor said. "I've only seen pictures of aliens, so they are not very real to me. But these creatures. Blood, green blood. And it looks as if they're all dead. Grey skin, pipestem limbs. Just from the pictures I've seen, is it possible that they could be . . ."

"Sulbani. You're right. One of the three intelligent races of aliens we've met in our expansion through the

57

galaxy—and the only ones who possessed an interstellar drive before we appeared on the scene. They already had their own little corner of the galaxy staked out and did not at all appreciate our arrival. We have been staying away from them and trying to convince them that we have no territorial ambitions on their planets. But some people are hard to convince. Some aliens even more so. The Sulbani are the worst. Suspicion is in their blood.

"All of the evidence seemed to point to their presence here on Trowbri, but I couldn't be absolutely sure until I came face to face with them. The use of high-frequency weapons is typical of them. You know that if you raise the pitch of sound, higher and higher, it becomes inaudible to human ears—though animals can still hear it. Raise it higher still and the animals can't hear it—but they feel it just as well as we can. Ultrasonics can do some strange things."

He kicked at one of the bent discs, not unlike a microwave aerial. "That was the first clue. They have ultrasonic projectors in the forest, broadcasting on a wavelength that is inaudible but causes a feeling of tension and uneasiness in most animals. That was the ghostly aura that kept people away from this plateau most of the time." He whistled a signal for the herd to assemble. "Animals, as well as men, will move away from the source, and they used it to chase some of the nastier wildlife towards us. When it didn't work and we came back, they sent in the more powerful stuff. Look at your shoes—and at this lantern."

Haydin gasped. The eyelets had vanished from his boots, and ragged pieces of lace hung from the torn openings. The lantern, like the metal equipment of the lost expedition, was squeezed and bent out of shape.

"Magnostriction," Bron said. "They were projecting a contracting and expanding magnetic field of an incredible number of gauss. The technique is used in factories for shaping metal, and it works just as well in the field. That, and these ultrasonic projectors to finish the job. Even a normal scan radar will give you a burn if you stand too close to it, and some ultrasonic wavelengths can turn water to vapour and explode organic material. That's what they did to your people who camped here. Swept in suddenly and caught them in the tents surrounded by their own equipment, which exploded and crunched and helped to wipe them out. Now let's get going."

"I don't understand what this means. I . . ."

"Later. We have to catch the one that got away."

On the side of the clearing where the machine had disappeared, they found a ragged length of black plastic. "Part of the skirt from the hovercraft," Bron said. "Confines the air and gives more lift. We'll follow them with this." He held out the fabric to Queeny and Jasmine and the other pigs that pressed up. "As you know, dogs track by odour that hangs in the air, and pigs have just as good noses or better. In fact, hunting pigs were used in England for years, and pigs are also trained to smell out truffles. There they go!"

Grunting and squealing, the leaders started away into the darkness. The two men stumbled after them, the rest of the pigs following. After a few yards, Haydin had to stop and bind his shoes together with strips from his handkerchief before he could go on. He held Bron's belt, and Bron had his fingers hooked into the thick bristles that formed a crest on Curly's spine, and in this way they pushed through the forest. The hovercraft had to go through open country, or their nightmare run would have been impossible.

When a darker mass of mountains loomed ahead, Bron whistled the herd to him. "Stay," he ordered. "Stay with Queeny. Curly, Moe, and Jasmine—with me."

They went more slowly now, until the grassland died away in a broken scree of rock at the foot of a nearly vertical cliff. To their left they could make out the black gorge of the river and hear it rushing by below.

"You told me those things can't fly," Haydin said.

"They can't. Jasmine, follow the trail."

The little pig, head up and sniffing, trotted steadily across the broken rock and pointed to the bare side of the cliff.

7

"COULD there possibly be a concealed entrance here?" Haydin asked, feeling the rough texture of the rock.

"There certainly could be—and we have no time to go looking for the key. Get behind those rocks, way over there, while I open this thing up."

He took blocks of a clay-like substance from his pack—a plastic explosive—and placed them against the rock, where they remained, over the spot that Jasmine had indicated. Then he pushed a fuse into the explosive, pulled the igniter—and ran. He had just thrown himself down with the others when flame ripped the sky and the ground heaved under them; a spatter of rocks fell on all sides.

They ran forward through the dust and saw light spilling out through a tall crevice in the rock. The boars threw themselves against it and it widened. Once through, they saw that a metal door was fastened to a section of rock and could swing outward to give access to the large cavern they were standing in. Bron bit his lip and examined the tunnel that ran down into the heart of the mountain.

"What next?" Governor Haydin asked.

"That's what I'm concerned about. At night, and out in the open, I'll back my boars against the Sulbani—or against human beings, for that matter. But these tunnels are a death trap for them. Even their speed won't protect them against gunfire. So let's even the odds. Everyone— back flat against this wall."

The Governor obeyed quickly enough, but it took a bit of tail pulling and two well-placed kicks to get the excited boars to obey. Only after they were all in position did Bron throw the switch on the wall of the entrance chamber of the tunnel. A large, inset metal door moved slowly upward—and laser beams hissed through the expanded opening.

"The hovercraft hangar," Bron whispered. "Looks as if some of them are still in there."

The boars didn't need orders. They waited, trembling with repressed energy, until the gap had widened enough to admit them. Then they struck at once, twin furies.

"Don't damage the gun!" Bron shouted as the laser beam fired again, wildly, then vanished. There were loud crunching sounds from inside.

"We can go in now," Bron said.

Inside the tool-lined room they found the body of only a single Sulbani. He must have been a mechanic, since the torn skirt had been removed from the hovercraft and a new one was ready to be fitted into place. Bron stepped over the corpse and picked up the laser rifle.

"Have you ever shot one of these?" he asked.

"No, but I'm willing to learn."

"Some other time. I'm an expert marksman with this particular weapon and I will be happy to prove it. Stáy here."

"No."

"That's your choice. Stay behind me, then, and maybe I can get you a weapon too. Let's move fast while we can still make some use of surprise."

Cautiously, flanked by the two boars, he moved down the well-lit cavern, and Haydin followed close behind. Trouble came at the first tunnel crossing. When they were about twenty yards from the other tunnel, a Sulbani leaped out suddenly, with his gun poised and ready to fire. Bron snapped a single shot from his waist, without appearing to aim, and the alien collapsed, motionless, on the tunnel floor.

"Go get them!" he shouted, and the boars plunged forward, one to each opening of the cross tunnel. Bron fired over them, into the tunnel mouths, until the air cracked and glowed with the discharge of the laser. The two men ran forward, but when they reached the cross tunnel the battle was over. Moe had a burn along one side—which did not slow him down, though it did make his temper worse. He rooted, snorting like a steam engine, in the temporary barricade, tossing boxes and furniture over his head.

"Here's your gun," Bron said, picking up an undamaged laser rifle. "I'll set it on maximum discharge, single shot. Just aim it and pull the trigger. And let's go. They know we're in now, but luckily they were not prepared for a battle inside their own hideout."

They ran, counting on speed and shock to get them through, stopping only when they encountered resistance. As they passed one tunnel mouth they heard distant shouting, and Bron skidded to a stop and called to the others.

"Hold it. In here. Those sound like human voices."

The metal door was set into solid rock; but the laser beam turned the lock to a molten puddle, and Bron pulled the door open.

"I was so sure we would never be found—that we would die here," Lea Davies said. She came out of the cell, half supported by a tall man with the same coppery red hair.

"Huw Davies?" Bron asked.

"The same," he said, "but let's keep the introductions until later. When they brought me in here I saw a good bit of the layout. The most important thing is a central control room. Everything operates from there—even their power plant is right next to it. And they have communication equipment."

"I'm with you," Bron said. "If we take that, we can cut off all the power and make them work in the dark. My boars will like that. They'll cruise around and keep things stirred up until the militia arrives. We'll call the town from there."

Huw Davies pointed at the laser rifle Haydin held. "I'd like to borrow that for a while, Governor, if you would let me. I have a few scores I want to settle."

"It's all yours. Now show us the way."

The battle for the control room was a brief one—the boars saw to that. Most of the furniture was smashed up, but the controls appeared still to be in working order.

"You stand guard at the entrance, Huw," Bron said, "since I read Sulbani script and you probably don't." He mumbled to himself over the phonetic symbols, then smiled with satisfaction. " 'Lighting circuit'—that's all *that* can mean." He stabbed at a button, and all the lights went out.

"I hope that it's dark all over, not just here," Lea said weakly in the black depths of the room.

"Everywhere," Bron told her. "Now, the emergency lighting circuit for this room should be here." Blue bulbs, scattered over the ceiling, flickered and came to life. Lea sighed audibly. "I've really had just about enough excitement," she said.

The two boars were looking expectantly at Bron, a wicked red gleam in their eyes. "Go to it, boys," he said. "Just don't get hurt."

"Little chance of that," Huw said as the great beasts exploded out the doorway and vanished with a rapid thud of hooves. "I've seen how they operate, and I'm glad I'm not on the receiving end." A distant crashing and thin screams echoed his sentiments.

Governor Haydin looked around at the banks of instruments and controls. "Now," he said, "that the excitement and immediate danger are over for the moment, will someone please tell me what is happening here and what all *this* is about?"

"A mine," Huw said, pointing towards a tunnel diagram on the far wall of the room. "A uranium mine—all in secret, and it has been running for years. I don't know how they're getting the metal out, but they mine and partially refine it here, all with automatic machinery, and powder the slag and dump it into the river out there."

"I'll tell you what happens then," Bron said. "When they have a cargo, it's lifted off by spacer. The Sulbani have very big ideas about moving out of their area and controlling a bigger portion of space. But they are short of power metals, and Earth has been working hard to keep it that way. One of the reasons this planet was settled was that it is near the Sulbani sector and, while we didn't need the uranium, we didn't want it falling into the Sulbani's hands. The Patrol had no idea that they were getting their uranium from Trowbri—though they knew it was coming from somewhere—but it was a possibility. When the Governor, here, sent in his request for aid, it became an even stronger possibility."

"I still don't understand it," Haydin said. "We would have detected any ships coming to the planet; our radar functions well."

"I'm sure it functions fine—but these creatures have at least one human accomplice who sees to it that the landings are concealed."

"Human . . . !" Haydin gasped. Then he knotted his

fists at the thought. "It's not possible. A traitor to the human race. Who could it be?"

"That's obvious," Bron said, "now that you have been eliminated as a possibility."

"*Me!*"

"You were a good suspect—in the perfect position to cover things up; that's why I was less than frank with you. But you knew nothing about the hovercraft raid and would have been killed if I hadn't pulled you down, so that took you off the list of suspects. Leaving the obvious man: Reymon—the radio operator."

"That's right," Lea said. "He let me talk to Huw on the phone—and then he made me call you or he said he would have Huw killed. He didn't say why he wanted to see you, I didn't know . . ."

"You couldn't have." Bron smiled at her. "He isn't much of a killer and must have been following Sulbani instructions to get rid of me. He really earned his money by not seeing their ships on radar. And by making sure that the radio communication with Huw's party was cut off when the Sulbani attacked. He probably recorded the signals and gave the murderers an hour or two to do their work before he broadcast the radios' cutting off. That would have helped the mystery. And now, Governor, I hope you'll give a favourable report about this P.I.G. operation."

"The absolute best," Haydin said. He looked down at Jasmine, who had tracked them down and now lay curled up at his feet, chewing on a bar of Sulbani rations. "In fact, I'm almost ready to swear off eating pork for the rest of my life."

When the Commanding Officer had finished speaking there was a moment's silence before the graduating Cadets broke into frenzied cheering and clapping. They stopped instantly when the Commanding Officer raised his hand.

"I can understand your enthusiasm. It has been operations like this one that have made the name of the Porcine Interstellar Guard secretly famous across the entire galaxy. They do the job. However, to be a P.I.G. patrolman requires certain skills and attitudes. For instance, you have to like pigs. In our modern industrialized galaxy many people have never seen any animal up close, not to mention a pig, and I noticed that a number of you were less than enthusiastic in your clapping. To you I say—do not worry. Only volunteers are accepted for Special Assignments. And there are assignments enough for all. If machines mean more to you than animals, why, there are plenty of opportunities to use your skills. When I said machine *a picture flashed instantly to my mind, the picture of a distant planet named Slagter and what happened there not so very long ago. . . .*

The Man from R.O.B.O.T.

1

THE framework of the battered spaceship was still trembling from the impact of landing, when the cargo hatch squealed open. With deft mechanical speed a claw-equipped handling boom dropped a drawer-filled store counter down on to the parched soil, then whipped out a gaudy, well-patched canopy which it spread above it. Still working swiftly, it brought out chairs, boxes, robots, a water cooler, a cash register, a cuspidor and countless other devices.

Almost as a side thought, in the midst of all this scurried activity, a rattling metal ladder dropped from the hatch to the ground. Down this, dodging the rushing boom, climbed a man. He was dressed in a gaudy checked coverall and wore, at a rakish angle, a round-brimmed, ancient-style headpiece known as a "derby". Before he reached the ground he was sweating profusely. His name was Henry Venn, though his friends called him Hank.

Bone-dry dust spurted out as Henry trudged over to the long counter and dropped into the chair behind it. He flicked a switch and loud, brassy music blared out. As he drew a paper cupful of water from the cooler the music faded, to be replaced by a booming recording of his voice.

"Come get 'em, come buy 'em, come grab 'em—while they're hot, cold or just luke-warm. You will never again in your lifetime see machines, household appliances or robots like these, so BUY BUY BUY before they're all gone!"

All this high-pressured salesmanship and scurrying activity appeared highly out of place in the barren land-scape. The orange sun burned down, raising undulating heat-waves. The spaceship had landed at the very end of the spaceport, which was really just a cleared and fenced field. At the far end, barely visible through the shimmering air, were the tower and port facilities. The soil baked and nothing moved. Henry lifted his hat and wiped first his forehead with a handkerchief, then the hat's sweatband, before dropping the derby back into position. Bright music blasted from the speakers and was soaked up by the heat and endless silence.

Something moved at the far end of the field, then grew quickly in size, a billowing cloud of dust. It swept towards the grounded spaceship until a dark spot was visible at its base. There was a clanking roar and Henry shut his eyes as the cloud of dust swirled around him. When he opened them he saw that the dark spot had become a large man, riding a single-treaded vehicle that had slid to a stop at the ship. The man spoke clearly and precisely and there was no doubt about his meaning.

"Get into that ship and get out of here."

"I would be happy to oblige," Henry said, smiling warmly. "But I am afraid that I cannot. Cracked rocket tube liner."

There was a strained silence as each sized the other up. They were a study in contrasts. The man mounted on the trackcycle—a species of motorcycle, gyro-stabilized, with a powered track instead of wheels—was tall, spare, weather-beaten. He peered from under the shelter of his wide-brimmed hat and his right hand rested carefully on the butt of a worn pistol in a holster on his leg. He looked very efficient.

Henry Venn looked very inefficient. He was moon-faced and smiling, and unkind people had even called him pudgy. He slumped where the other man sat erect and the sweat-dampened, white-skinned hand that he reached out for the cup of water trembled ever so slightly.

"Have a drink?" he asked. "Good cold water. My name is Venn, Henry Venn, and my friends call me Hank. I'm afraid I didn't catch yours. Sheriff," he added, noticing the word on the gold badge pinned to the other's broad chest.

"Get your junk into the ship. Blast off from here. You got two minutes before I shoot you."

"I would love to oblige, believe me. But the cracked liner . . ."

"Put in a new one. Blast off from here."

"I would—if I had a spare. Which I don't. You don't happen to know if there is one here in the spaceport?"

"Blast off from here," the Sheriff said again, but his heart wasn't really in it this time. You could see that he was thinking about the tube liner and what had to be done to get the stranger and his ship offplanet. Henry took advantage of the momentary lull to press a switch, on the back of the counter, with his knee.

"Real Olde Rottgutt Whiskey, the best in the galaxy," a small robot shouted tinnily, springing to life on the top of the counter. It appeared to be constructed from sections of pipe and had large pliers for jaws. It held an amber bottle in its tong-like hands, which it thrust forwards towards the Sheriff.

The tall man reacted instantly, pulling out a long-barrelled gun and firing. There was a cloud of smoke and a loud bang and the bottle flew into fragments.

"Try to kill me, hey?" the Sheriff shouted, swinging the pistol towards the other man and pulling the trigger.

Henry did not move, nor did the smile leave his face. The gun clicked, then clicked again rapidly as the Sheriff pulled at the trigger. With a horrified look at the still placid Henry, he jammed the gun back into its holster, gunned his engine to life, then tore away in the centre of a growing cloud of dust.

"Now what was all that about?" Henry asked, apparently speaking to the thin air around him. The air answered back: a hoarse voice that whispered in his ear.

"The individual with the combustion-pellet weapon was intending to do you injury. This weapon is constructed of ferrous metals. I therefore generated an intense and localized magnetic field that kept the internal parts from moving and, therefore, the weapon from operating."

"He'll think something is phoney about that."

"Hardly. The records indicate that these weapons are prone to malfunctions. This malfunction is called a 'misfire'."

"I'll remember that," Henry said, taking a sip of water.

"You'll remember what?" a shrill voice asked from the other side of the counter.

Henry had to lean far forward to see the small boy who stood there, his head below the level of the counter top.

"I'll remember that you are my first customer on this fair planet, therefore you must receive the special First Customer prize."

He played a quick pattern on the keyboard inset before him, and a flap opened in the counter top. The pipe-limbed robot reached into the revealed opening and pulled out a foot-wide, candy-striped lollipop. He extended it towards the little boy, who eyed it suspiciously.

"What's that thing?"

"A particularly toothsome form of candy. You take the wooden part in one hand and stick the round part in your mouth."

The boy did this instantly and began crunching on the lollipop.

"Do you know who the man was who just left?" Henry asked.

"The sheriff." The words were mumbled around the dissolving sweet.

"Is that the only name he has?"

"Sheriff Mordret. The kids don't like him."

"I hardly blame them . . ."

"What's he eating?" a voice asked, and Henry turned to see a larger boy, a teenager, who had appeared as silently as the first.

"Candy. Would you like some? The first piece is free."

After a moment's consideration the boy nodded *yes.* Henry bent to a lower drawer in the counter so his face

72

would be concealed while he whispered. The boys could not hear him, but the tracking microphones of the ship picked his words up clearly.

"What's going on here? Where are these kids coming from? Are you asleep on the job?"

"Computers do not sleep," the projected voice of the ship said in his ear. "The boys are not armed and move very cautiously. It is my opinion they do not pose a threat. There are five more of them approaching the ship from different directions."

They came sidling up to the counter, one by one, and each accepted a free piece of candy. Henry pressed a key on the cash register and a bell rang, the drawer flew open and the little sign reading NO SALE appeared in the window.

"That's what it is so far, boys," he told them. "No sale. Not one. So what will it be—more candy? I have plenty here. Toys, books, you name it, I stock them all. Rush home and crack into your piggy banks and buy a mem-robot, a 2-way radio, a . . ."

"A gun?" the teenager asked hopefully. "I think I could use a gun."

"Robbie's getting big enough he's going to need a gun soon," a smaller boy said and the others nodded in agreement.

"Sorry, I don't stock guns," Henry said, which was an outright lie. "And even if I did I couldn't sell them to minors."

"I'll get a gun from my uncle when I want to," Robbie said, scowling fiercely.

The cash register jungled merrily for a few minutes as

73

the boys produced what small change they had in exchange for the assorted items that small boys always buy.

"Nice planet you got here," Henry said, pushing a stack of soundie comic books across the counter for Robbie's inspection. There was the sound of tiny explosions, bits of dialogue, and the roar of miniature rocket engines heard as he flipped through the pages.

"Not bad if you like cows," he mumbled, more interested in the new comics.

"Get many visitors here?"

"None. People here on Slagter don't like strangers."

"Well, you must get some. One at least. I know the Galactic Census came through this system awhile back. I think a Commander Sergejev was in charge."

"Oh, yeah, him." Tiny, savage screams sounded from the open pages. "But he just landed and went right away again . . ."

Robbie broke off and cocked his head to one side. He closed the magazine and slid a coin across to pay for it, then turned away. The other boys were starting away with their purchases too. In a few moments they were gone.

2

"And what is all that about?" Henry asked aloud.

"A vehicle is approaching from the direction of the spaceport," the computer said. "The boys' hearing is superior to yours and they detected it earlier."

"They're younger, so they can hear higher frequencies,"

Henry grumbled. "And I can hear it now too. And even see the dust with my fine, superior 20-20 vision. Wise guy computer."

"I simply state the facts," it answered, with mechanical smugness.

The new arrival was a half-track truck that roared up and slid to a screeching stop. Henry sighed as the resultant dust cloud rolled over him. Did everyone on Slagter drive in this headlong way?

A man jumped down from the cab, and he could have been a brother or a near relative of the Sheriff. Here again was the wide hat and steely gaze, leather-tanned skin and ready gun.

"Howdy stranger," Henry said, once more staring down a cavernous gun barrel. "My name's Henry Venn, but my friends call me Hank. And your name must be . . . ?"

A surly scowl was the only answer Henry received to this friendly question. He smiled in return and tried again.

"Yes, well, no point in going into that now. Is there anything I can do for you? Sell you a little winged transistor radio that will follow you everywhere and sing sweet music into your ear night and day . . ."

"Does a 30-M3 tube liner fit the jets on that bucket of bolts you fly?" the man asked.

"It sure does," Henry said brightly. "Do you know where I can get one?"

"Here," the newcomer said, pulling the tall ceramic tube from the back of the truck and dropping it on to the counter. "That will be exactly 467 credits."

Henry nodded and rang open the register. "I can give you 3·25 in cash, and my check for the balance."

75

"Cash on the line."

"Then I'm afraid that you will have to wait until I sell some of my high-class wares, because I'm a little short on cash at this moment."

The man's eyes narrowed and his fingers tapped at the butt of his gun.

"I tell you what I'll do. I'll barter. Trade you this tube liner for a mess of guns, rifles, grenades, ammo . . ."

"I'm sorry, but I do not stock lethal weapons. However, I have some first-class robots for all uses."

"Fighting and killing robots?"

"No, not that kind. But I can sell you a bodyguard robot that will prevent anything or anybody from hurting you. What about that?"

"If it works, it's a deal. Trot it out."

Henry tapped a fast pattern on his control keys. The robot would be an ordinary general purpose type, but its responses would be specially programmed for this job. He instructed the computer as to just what he wanted. Less than ten seconds later a gleaming, manlike robot appeared in the open hatch above and rushed headlong down the ladder. It sprang to the ground at the bottom and rendered a snappy salute.

"What kind of robot are you?" Henry asked.

"I am a bodyguard robot. I will do everything in my power to keep he, she or it that I am guarding from harm."

"It is a he, and there he is. Guard him."

The robot ran in a quick circle about his new master and, seeing no immediate dangers, stood, humming alertly, at his side. The man looked the machine suspiciously up and down.

"Doesn't look like much. How do I know it will work?"

"I shall demonstrate."

Henry took a long-bladed hunting knife from one of the drawers and grasped it firmly by the hilt. Then, with an unexpected leap he hurled himself across the counter shouting "Kill! Kill!"

The action was over before the startled man could draw his gun. The robot sprang into position, grabbed and twisted. The knife spun away into the dust and Henry was flat on his back on the ground, with one of the robot's feet planted firmly on his chest.

"It's a deal," the man said, letting his gun slide back into the holster. "Now get that liner in and haul out of here before sundown, or you won't live to see the dawn."

"How nice of you to let me know. But one formality if you please. I'll need your name for the bill of sale and robot registration," Henry said, stylus poised over his sales book.

The man registered all the visible effects of acute suffering: furrowed brow, worried look, deep scowl, twitching fingers.

"What you want my name for?" he asked, his words fairly dripping with suspicion.

"A matter of legality, sir. Without your name this bill of sale is not final and you do not officially own that fine robot that is now guarding you with every molecule of its steel being. That robot could be taken away, once more exposing you to the rigours of solitude . . ."

"Silas Enderby," he whispered hoarsely, sweating and shaking as he forced the words reluctantly through his

77

lips. As though ashamed of this admission he hurled himself into his truck and kicked it to life.

"Stranger and stranger," Henry said, brushing the dust from his clothes as he watched the half-track speed off with his robot. "Poor Silas acted as though speaking his name aloud were taboo. What strange custom can we have run up against here?" He mused over the thought but no brilliant answers sprang to mind, so he abandoned it for the moment and spoke to the computer. "Do you believe the boy's story that Sergejev left this planet?"

"Highly doubtful," the computer said. "The odds are exactly 97·346 to 1 against it. A Commander in the Galactic Census does not leave without his ship."

"And his ship is buried right here under this field. How far are we from it?"

"The concealed ship is fifteen feet below the surface and exactly 135 feet 6 inches north-east of your right toe. I fixed its location precisely before we landed through an exchange of information with its computer. I felt that suspicion would be attached if the landing was effected directly over the burial site."

"A wise decision, I'm sure. How is the tunnel coming?"

"It is completed. I sent the boring machine down through the landing leg and it reached the entrance port of the other ship exactly 3·86 minutes ago. It has now returned and is digging a secondary tunnel to your counter."

"Let me know when it arrives. And this time I sincerely hope that you will do something spectacular in the way of reinforcing the tunnel walls?"

There was a momentary silence before the ship spoke

again—signifying a rapid search of countless memory files, followed by some equally speedy deductions.

"It is my conclusion that you are referring, in a negative and/or satirical manner, to the affair on Gilgamesh IV where there was a minor tunnel cave-in. I have explained before that this was wholly accidental, due to . . ."

"I've heard your explanation. I just want you to assure me that it won't happen again."

"All precautions have been taken," the ship answered in what could not possibly have been a hurt voice because, after all, it was only a machine.

Henry drew another paper cup of water and tapped the tube liner: it rang musically. The robots could install it in an hour, but if he took out the winch and pretended to do it himself he could stretch the operation until dark. He had to find a way to gain more time on the planet: he doubted if he could possibly finish his assignment before the following morning.

"Tunnel completed," the ship whispered in his ear.

"Good. Get ready. Here I come."

In case he were under observation he played the role broadly. He drank from the cup again and put it down near the edge of the counter. Then he yawned, tapping his mouth with his hand to show that he was yawning, not just seeing how wide he could open his jaw, then stretched widely. When he did this his hand knocked the cup to the ground. He looked down at it, then bent to pick it up. As he did so he was below the level of the counter and out of sight of anyone at the other end of the field.

The back of the counter opened wide and he crawled into it. As he crept into it he pushed past himself and crawled out of it. The he that came out wasn't the same he that went in, but was a humanoid robot whose plasti-flesh was modelled after his features, right down to the last dewlap and mole. The robot picked up the paper cup and straightened up, seating itself in the chair. To the uninformed observer Henry was still seated, waiting patiently for business to materialize.

He was doing nothing of the sort. He was climbing down a ladder into a well-lit tunnel some twenty feet under the ground.

3

"THERE seems to be a bit of improvement over the tunnel that caved in," Henry said.

"That is true," the ship said, speaking through the mouth of a small multi-legged robot that was holding a sign in its claw hands. There was an arrow painted on the sign, and below the arrow was printed TO THE BURIED SHIP. Henry went in that direction.

It is of course impossible for a ship's computer to feel guilt. But perhaps this one felt that it had not performed adequately the previous time when the fused earth tunnel had collapsed at one spot. This tunnel was completely lined with stainless steel plates, welded together and reinforced. The top was high enough for Henry to walk upright, and inset glow tubes lit his way. Soft music sounded from hidden speakers as he trod on the ridged, slip-proof flooring. This tunnel bent sharply where it entered the main tunnel which had been dug from beneath his ship. A welding robot stepped aside to let him pass, then pointed in the right direction with its torch-tipped arm.

". . . the buried ship . . . is that way . . ." it said in a flat, monochromatic voice.

"Not bad, not bad at all," Henry said, particularly delighted by a projected photomural of a winter forest that covered one wall. The tunnel ended at the curved metal flank of the buried spaceship, with the airlock neatly centred before him. A heavy-duty robot was leaning on a high-intensity spark drill that was eating a hole through the hull.

"You forgot to mention that we had to break in," Henry said.

"You neglected to ask," the ship said, speaking through the drilling robot. "The computer in this ship is of a very low order and incapable of much rational thought. It supplied navigational instructions upon request because it was programmed to do so, but it refuses to open the lock because we do not know the proper keying phrase. It is therefore necessary to interrupt its control."

At that moment the drill holed through. The robot ran the bit as far forward as it would go to make sure that the opening was clear, then drew it out. A tiny robot hummed down the corridor from the ship. It was no thicker than a man's finger, and not unlike a mechanical centipede with its numerous legs. A wire trailed behind it and, when it scuttled up the wall of the buried spacer, Henry saw a jewel-like TV eye on its front, just over a wicked-looking cutting beak. It went straight to the hole and vanished into it, trailing the wire after.

"What's that for?"

"Direct control," the ship answered through the welding robot as it passed on its way back down the tunnel. "I am disconnecting the computer and taking over."

Apparently it was. Within a minute hidden motors hummed and the airlock swung open. Henry found the wire where it came through the hole and followed it to the control room. The tiny cable led to a small inspection hatch that had been pulled from the computer, and he had a quick glimpse of cut wires inside, with the multi-legged robot hanging like a mechanical leech from a terminal strip. The air was pure, the ship was clean; there was no sign of human habitation.

"What have you found out?" he asked.

The ship's computer answered, though he knew it was his own ship speaking.

"The last entry in the log is over one standard year ago. 372 days to be exact. It reads, 'Landed. 1645 hours.' "

"Not very communicative, our Commander Sergejev. He must have landed, made the log entry, then gone out to begin his survey. And never returned. Is there anything more in the memory bank?"

"Just a series of radio warnings the ship issued, not to molest government property; that was three days after the landing. We may assume that this was when the ship was buried."

"We may. We can guess that something nasty happened to the Commander—which must be easy enough on this peace-loving planet. The party or parties concerned couldn't break into the ship—so they buried it to remove the evidence. So, now what?"

"I would suggest a return to the counter. A vehicle is approaching rapidly."

"Vision!"

The navigation screen lit up as the computer piped in a signal from one of its pickups. There was the familiar dust cloud approaching at its usual headlong pace.

"I'll never get back before they arrive, so let's have the robot stand in this once."

"It is not programmed for more than simple movements and expressions."

"Then cut me into its voice circuit, that should be simple enough."

It was. The humanoid robot sat and grinned as the truck slid to a stop and a group of men jumped down.

"What will you have, gentlemen?" Henry said. "I stock only the finest of wares."

The computer taped his words and delayed them by 100 milliseconds so that it could programme the robot's jaw motions to match the sounds. The deception appeared to work, because the Slagterans came up to the counter and scowled down at the seated figure. One of them was the Sheriff, and the others were built and dressed like him.

"You been asking questions?" the Sheriff said.

"Who—me?" Henry answered, and the robot's finger pointed dutifully to its own chest.

"Yes you. You been asking about Commander Sergejev?"

As he said this, words appeared on the screen over his image, moving smoothly from left to right.

ONE OF THE MEN IS NOW MOVING AROUND BEHIND THE
COUNTER . . . HE HAS WHAT APPEARS TO BE A BLUNT
WEAPON IN HIS RAISED HAND.

"I don't recall mentioning the name," Henry said,
then put his hand over the mike. "If they want to cause
trouble—let them. We may find out more that way."

"I think you have," the Sheriff said, leaning close. "In
fact, I know you have."

YOU HAVE BEEN STRUCK ON THE REAR OF THE CRANIUM
the moving words said, and the image shifted to show the
Henry-robot falling forward across the counter.

"Ohhhhh," Henry moaned, then was silent.

"You are now disconnected," the computer said.

"Let's get some bugs on the truck, lots of them.
Complete coverage of facilities and channels."

The Slagterans moved swiftly—almost professionally—
in disposing of their supposedly stunned and unconscious
prisoner. Two men took the Henry-robot under the
armpits and pulled him away from the desk. A third man
then grabbed up his ankles and they rushed him to the
back of the truck and threw him inside. The sheriff was
already in the cab gunning the engine and, as the men
jumped in and the last foot cleared the ground, he sent
the truck leaping ahead. Scant seconds had passed from
the bludgeoning to the kidnapping. They had moved fast.

Yet the robots had moved faster. While nerve impulses
move at the sluggish rate of 300 feet per second, electricity
travels at the speed of light. Which, at the last reckoning,
went 186,326 miles in that same second of time. So, while
the men were just reaching for the slumped figure,
electronic commands had already opened bins and

lockers in the ship. By the time the men had picked up their limp burden, hundreds of robots were already rushing to obey commands. The biggest of them was the size of a button, the smallest the size of an ant. And all of them were under the direct control of the ship's computer. Down the hollow landing leg they streamed, out through the tunnel and up into the counter. A hatch on the side facing the truck sprang open and the twinkling, scurrying horde rushed out. Some of them climbed up the half-track treads, others sprang into the body in mighty leaps, while still others energized minuscule jets and flew to their objective. By the time the Slagterans appeared all of the robots were out of sight.

"Get me a view from the front of the truck," Henry said, leaning back in the pilot's chair, prepared to enjoy his own kidnapping in comfort.

The screen before him blurred and cleared, showing a close-up of rushing dirt, much dust, and little else.

"Too low. Don't you have an eye up on the cab?"

The scene shifted again, to a point further up the truck, where there was a fine view of the spaceport buildings rushing towards them. The buildings streamed by as the truck turned and tore headlong down a rutted dirt road.

"Their paving leaves a lot to be desired. I can understand now why all their vehicles have treads. I hope that you are taking advantage of this journey to bug all the riders in the truck?"

"This has already been done. At the present moment there are a minimum of six pickups on each individual. That number will be increased dependent upon the length of this present trip."

85

"The longer the ride, the buggier they get. I wonder where they are headed? They've turned away from town, haven't they?"

"They have."

The road turned and twisted, and suddenly moving forms were visible through the dust ahead. Without slowing speed the Sheriff pulled off the road and swung wide through the shrub to avoid the obstacle. The cross-country track was, if anything, smoother than the road, so the pickups presented a clear picture of the herd of milling animals that they passed. Henry looked on in wonderment at the rolling eyes and heaving flanks, at the great spread of needle-sharp horns each animal bore.

"What in the name of sanity are those evil-looking beasts?" Henry asked, and the ship's computer searched the infinite resources of its memory files and produced the answer in a few milliseconds.

"A sub-order of the Earth specie *bos domesticus*. This animal has been back-bred from the common short-horn beef cattle to recreate the longhorn, once common in a certain portion of Earth titled the United States, particularly a sub-geographical category of mythological interest called Texas. The longhorns originated in Spain . . ."

"That will do nicely. Any more detail would only give me a headache. So these violent-looking beasts must be the basis of Slagter economy. Very interesting. See if you can't plant a bug on that surly individual on the track-cycle who is accompanying the flock."

"Flock is the collective term of a group of birds. The correct term applied to cattle is *herd* . . ."

"Were you working while you gave me the lecture?"

"The ordered operation is complete."

Sudden gunfire interrupted, followed by a sharp explosion. The screen was filled with an exploding cloud of dust, then it went blank.

4

"I DON'T suppose you could tell me what happened," Henry said in a most sarcastic manner.

"I will be happy to tell you," the ship answered, ignoring his tone of voice. "The half-track was first fired upon and then it hit a landmine. I will switch the view to a spy-eye above the scene."

It was a scene of absolute confusion. No one in the half-track seemed to have been badly hurt when it overturned since all of them were now concealed behind it and firing away lustily at another group of men. These men, who were mounted on trackcycles, appeared to have been riding with the herd of cattle. They had deserted their charges now and sought protection behind irregularities in the ground so that they could fire back. Small arms fire crackled, the cattle bellowed and milled about and general confusion ruled. The Henry robot lay crumpled in the dust like a discarded doll.

There was a brief lull in the firing—perhaps while they reloaded their weapons—and a white flag appeared from behind the overturned vehicle. A few shots ripped through the cloth before the shooting stopped completely. One of the attackers called out:

"Throw down your guns, because you cattle rustlers are going to hang before sundown."

"What rustlers?" a peevish voice called back. "This is the sheriff here. *Your* sheriff, elected this month. Why you shoot at us and blow up the truck?"

"Why you try to steal our cows!"

"We don't want your cows. We got a prisoner here who we're taking in. The offworlder."

There was mumbled consultation after this before the spokesman shouted again. "Let's see him."

Henry saw himself raised above the armoured side of the truck and winced, waiting for the bullets to sink in. Nothing happened.

"All right, so you're the sheriff. You can go. But don't try to rustle cows again, hear?"

"How can we go? You knocked out our vehicle."

After much shouting back and forth the two groups emerged, keeping their hands near their weapons, and looked over the damage. It did not appear to be major; apparently the half-track had been built to take this kind of punishment. They tied ropes to it and managed to rock it back on to its tracks by pulling with their trackcycles. The sheriff's party climbed back in and the two groups parted with many a glowering look.

"You could never accuse them of being friendly," Henry said as the ride continued.

Pens were now visible ahead and the truck was speeding past great numbers of cattle that had been assembled in separated areas. A road led between the pens and ended at a large and windowless building. The truck made its usual sliding stop and, when the resulting dust cloud had cleared, a group of men was revealed, gathered about a locked door.

It was the most locked door that Henry had ever seen in his life, and he looked at it with mystified awe. There were a dozen or more hasps set along the edge of the door, from which dangled padlocks of various sizes and shapes. The reason for this odd construction was only apparent after the newcomers had joined the waiting men for an important discussion. They did not stand close, but rather gathered in a circle, well apart from each other, hands comfortably near the guns that they all wore. An agreement was quickly reached—Henry did not pay attention to the conversation since the computer was recording it and could play it back at any time—and, one by one, they sidled over to the locked door.

And each unlocked a lock, just one lock.

"Not very trusting are they?" Henry said. "Apparently every man has a key to his own lock, so they all have to be present to open that door. What secrets can be concealed behind such elaborate precautions?"

"It appears obvious from the location of this building that it contains . . ."

"Enough. Allow a little mystery in a man's life. You are too cold-minded and calculating, computer. Haven't you ever wished to experience the joys of anticipation, fear, doubt, curiosity . . . ?"

"I am perfectly content without them, thank you. The satisfactions of knowledge, and the operations of logic, suffice for a machine."

"Yes, I imagine they do. But our friends are moving. The door is unlocked and they are carrying my pseudo-self into the building. Switch to a bug inside so we can see what mysteries lurk there."

The optical pickup must have been located on one of the men's hats, because the picture, though bobbing with his footsteps, was high up and clear.

"A slaughterhouse," Henry said. "Of course."

It was more than just a slaughterhouse; it was a completely automated operation from the time the animals were herded into the pens at the far end of the building. From here the beef cattle were moved with electric prods into separate walkways. Soothing mists of ataraxic, sedative and hypnotic drugs filled the air so that the happy beasts strolled happily into their sunset. Once transformed from beast to beef, instantaneously and painlessly, they were carried forward on sort of a reverse assembly line. Unlike copters or cars, which were assembled from parts and emerged complete, the sides of beef were quickly disassembled to their component parts and whisked off to the freezers. The entire operation was swift, sterile, foolproof—and completely automatic. Not one human being was visible behind the sealed glass partition. The disassembly lines moved forward steadily and endlessly without a human hand to guide them.

Yet there had to be some control centre where the data storage and operating computers were located, and this appeared to be where the cowboy kidnappers were headed. The Sheriff pulled open the heavy bolt that sealed a metal door, and the Henry-robot was carried inside. Not all the men entered and the screen jumped dizzily as the computer shifted pickups to get a better image.

Things moved fast. The pictured scene flicked back to

the first pickup as the men came out and the Sheriff sealed the door again. They had left the robot behind.

"What is the point of all this?" Henry asked, and had the answer even as he spoke the words.

The Henry-robot opened its eyes and sat up. Its gaze went down to the fetter secured about its ankle, then along the length of chain that led to a heavy eye bolted to the wall. There were computer components and data storage tanks on all sides, and a door in the far wall through which a man was emerging, still rubbing the sleep from his eyes. He stopped abruptly when he saw the newcomer.

"At last—one of you alone!" he bellowed, and dived forward. His fingers locked about the Henry-robot's throat and clamped tight. "Release me or I'll kill you!"

The viewscreen, using the robot's eyes as pickups, was filled with the angry face of the newcomer. His large black beard waggled with his exertions and his bald head gleamed. Henry signalled the computer so that he could speak through the robot once again.

"Commander Sergejev, I presume."

"You've got a strong neck," Sergejev muttered, squeezing harder although his hands were getting tired.

"Very glad to meet you, Commander, although I would prefer if you shook my hand instead of my neck. If you will look down you will notice that I am a prisoner, chained just as you are, so that throttling me will avail you nothing."

Sergejev dropped his hands and stepped back. There was a chain leading from his ankle to the room he had just emerged from.

"Who are you—and what are you doing here?" Sergejev asked.

"My name is Henry Venn, my friends call me Hank, and I am a poor pedlar of robust robots, unfairly assaulted by the thugs who inhabit this planet."

"I can almost believe your story—because they got me the same way. But still, there's something funny about your neck . . ."

Once more computer-printed words moved across the image on the screen.

ROOMS SEARCHED AND ONLY ONE BUG FOUND . . . THIS HAS BEEN DISCONNECTED AND I AM NOW FEEDING IT SIMULATED INFORMATION FROM THE MEMORY BANK.

"Very good," Henry said. "We can lower the disguise for the moment. Stand me up." Commander Sergejev stepped back and raised his fists at the sudden action.

"There is nothing to fear," Henry said, speaking through the robot. "You are Commander Sergejev of the Galactic Census, first reported missing eight standard months ago. I have been sent to locate you."

"Well, you have found me all right, but other than that you don't seem to be doing so well."

"Do not let appearances fool you, Commander. My card."

The robot opened its mouth and reached in to extract an identity card which it handed to the man.

"That's a good trick," he said. "It's not even wet."

"There is no reason for it to be. What you are speaking to now is a robot duplicate of myself. I am at the spaceport. If you will be so kind as to examine the card . . ."

"R.O.B.O.T.! What is that supposed to mean? This

stupid robot with the big mouth gives me a card saying it is a robot!"

"Read the fine print below, if you please," Henry said patiently.

Sergejev held the card at arm's length and read slowly.

"Robot Obtrusion Battalion—Omega Three. Henry Venn, Commanding Officer." He looked around suspiciously. "So where is the battalion? What kind of a joke is this?"

"No joke at all. I can assume that you have access to classified documents in your work as a senior officer of the Galactic Census?"

"If I do, I'm not telling you."

"There is no need. You will know that the Patrol cannot possibly handle all the problems of law enforcement that arise within its sphere of influence. Most of the planets settled by humans do a good job of policing themselves— but not all of them. The Patrol has more calls for aid than it can possibly handle with its present number of armed spacecraft. Nor is armed threat always the answer to every problem. Therefore a number of other special units are being activated."

"Yes, I've heard about P.I.G., the Porcine Interstellar Guard. You don't have any pigs with you, do you?" Sergejev asked, hopefully. "You can't beat pigs for taking care of a tough job."

"Sorry, no pigs, but I think you will find that R.O.B.O.T. will do its job equally well. I work alone, but I am aided by the most sophisticated computers, detectors, apparatus and . . ."

"Read me the inventory later. Get me out of here first."

"Soon, Commander, soon," Henry said, soothingly. "But isn't there a little problem to be solved first? Like why you have been made a prisoner—and what you are doing here? I can take you out of here easily enough, but the planetary situation remains unchanged."

"Let it!" Sergejev paced back and forth, his chain clanking behind him. "This planet is a rustic deadend and it should remain that way. A perversion of the go-it-alone frontier spirit, where every man is an individualist and will kill everyone else to prove it."

"It doesn't sound healthy," Henry mused.

"Who cares? The Forbrugeners don't care—and this planet used to belong to them. They originally settled it as a colony. They are the fourth planet from this sun, the next one out."

"I know I traced you that far. They told me you had come here to Slagter even though they had warned you not to."

"I should have listened. But I took my Census Oath seriously then. That was before I was locked up in this slaughterhouse for a year. After the pressures of the highly industrialized life on Forbrugen, the settlers who came here were happy to make a new way of life for themselves. They have almost completely cut themselves off from their parent world and have created a society which, I am forced to admit, is about the nastiest I have ever encountered in my sixty-seven years of census service."

"Please tell me about it."

"How much do you know already?" Sergejev asked, still suspicious. His imprisonment in the mechanized meat-market had done nothing good for his humour.

94

"Just the surface facts. Forbrugen is a highly mechanized world and Slagter performs a very important role in its economy. This planet is ideal for the raising of beef cattle, and apparently nothing else is done here. The beef is frozen, loaded into cargo shells, then lifted into orbit by space tugs. The unmanned shells are launched into an orbit by the tugs, towards the future position of Forbrugen. These interplanetary meatlockers take anywhere from six to ten months for the trip, depending upon the relative position of the planets. The length of the journey doesn't matter because there are always a number of cargoes in the pipeline. About the time one is launched here another is picked up and slowed by tugs at the other end. A steady supply of meat is always on hand."

"Do you know about the treaty?"

"Yes. The Slagterans load the meat into the shells and their responsibility ends there. The Forbrugen ships deliver all the consumer goods that are needed here, pick up the full shells, return the empty ones—and never set foot on the planet's surface. They supply all the consumer goods the Slagterans need, but otherwise have no contact with them at all. The entire arrangement seems straightforward enough—until you take a close look at this planet."

"*You* can say that—hah! Only I, Sergejev, know the complete truth about this planet and it is enough to turn the blood to ice. One time I, like you, was an innocent and even laughed when they told me about Slagter. . . ."

5

"It is what you might call a . . . special relationship," the official behind the desk said, tapping his fingers nervously on the desk top.

"So?" Commander Sergejev answered, trying not to sound bored. Behind the other's back a great window opened out on to the main Forbrugen spaceport. He could see his own spacer, polished and sleek, with the refuelling hoses just being disconnected. He was eager to leave. Taking the Forbrugen census had been a piece of cake, almost too easy. The planet was highly organized and centralized, with computerized records on all its citizenry. He had spent some days investigating the system until he had assured himself that everyone on the planet was in the records. Taking the census had then consisted of asking the computer how many people there were on the planet. A microsecond later the figure had been printed on the readout and he had copied it into his own forms. Big deal. The next planet, Slagter, promised to offer at least some minor problems, so should be a good deal more interesting than this one. Sergejev realized that the official was still talking and he made some effort to listen.

". . . almost all of our meat, the largest single source of protein for our population. While we realize that the Slagterans have developed some, what shall we call them?—*exotic* customs—there is really nothing at all that we can do about it. Strangers are not welcome there and our people never set foot on the planetary surface. So we can offer you no assistance if there should be any trouble—"

"Trouble the census expects," Commander Sergejev said jumping to his feet and throwing back his shoulders. "Assistance we do not need. If that is all, I will be getting on with my task. Neither rain nor meteor storm nor gloom of night shall stay the census-takers from making their counts."

"Ahh, yes, I'm sure that is true. Good luck then, Commander." The official extended his hand and shook hands in a most feeble way. The Commander, always a man of action, squeezed hard in his usual manner, feeling the other's little bones crunch and slide across one another; then he turned on his heel and left.

It was a brisk day and he was glad to be leaving. His heavy boots thudded on the ferrocrete as he stalked quickly to his ship. The departure papers were all in order: he scrawled his name and pocketed his own copy. This ceremony performed he closed the airlock behind him and went to his bridge. The bright eye of the ship's computer followed him as he sat down and strapped himself in. Frowning with strict concentration he reached for the controls.

SET COURSE FOR SLAGTER he scrawled on the navpanel, then waited for the *ready* light to blink on. As soon as it did he pressed the button labelled *takeoff*. The ship did. Computerization had taken a lot of the work out of piloting and navigation.

Once the ship was in orbit he hurried to the game room, rubbing his hands together with anticipation. For the last few days, when not actively engaged with his work, he had been thinking about the Second Battle of Spica III. Military historians considered this a classic encounter in which the Denebians *had* to lose. All theorists agreed on this. Commander Sergejev did not. He would refight the battle and this time the Denebians would win.

The game room was a special modification of his own, with a feedout from the ship's computer. All the great military engagements of history—and most of the minor ones—were on record in the computer's memory. These battles could be refought in the game room, with the computer taking one side and the Commander the other. With the additional point of interest that the battles could be changed while they were being fought and did not have to follow the original pattern. In this fashion Sergejev passed days and weeks, stopping only when the computer ordered him to—it monitored his metabolism—for food and sleep.

"The Second Battle of Spica III," he shouted as he entered and instantly the air darkened and filled with the symbols of ships in space, a glowing sun in the background. He dropped into his control console with a grim smile and began to issue his first orders.

Nor did he stop until they were in orbit around Slagter and the computer had announced this fact seven times. Getting no response it cut the games circuits and light flooded back into the room as the spacewrecks and gutted suns faded from sight. Sergejev looked up, blinking.

"Now you quit—just when I was winning!" he shouted.

"You have lost this battle nineteen times in a row," the computer announced calmly. "My analysis of the present encounter is that you will lose this time too. We are in orbit about Slagter."

"I could have won," Sergejev muttered as he went to change into a fresh uniform and smeared dip cream on his whiskery jaw. "I would have won."

Landing was accomplished with the same ease as takeoff by the computer. There was a radio beacon to guide the Forbrugen ships and they followed it down for a landing on a dusty and deserted spaceport. The Commander called the control tower on the normal spaceport frequency and received no answer. Frowning, he used the other ship frequencies and finally the emergency band. There was no response.

"Inhospitable," he growled, "but the census cannot be ignored." He polished the visor of his cap on his sleeve, then put the cap on—at precisely the correct angle prescribed in the book of regulations. His identification was in his inner pocket and his ceremonial sidearm snapped on to loops on his belt. He was ready. The census would not be ignored.

Halfway down the gangway to the ground—and already beginning to sweat inside his heavy uniform—he saw the dust cloud hurrying his way. He waited on the last step to see what kind of reception he was going to receive.

It was not quite what he expected. A ground car of some kind, driven by a mixture of wheels and tracks, skidded to a shuddering stop before him. There were two men in it and both stood up and began firing at him, one with a pistol and the other with an automatic weapon.

Trained reflex took over. Even as his conscious mind was recovering from the shock and beginning to shout curses at the assassins his combat training sent him diving forward to the ground, rolling to one side. Even as he rolled he was drawing his ceremonial pistol which— ceremonial or no—he always kept carefully cleaned and loaded. It was an old-fashioned large-bore weapon that fired rocket-propelled explosive slugs.

Though outgunned and surprised, the Commander was a much better shot. Bullets hit all around him in the dirt and clanged off the gangway, doing little or no harm.

His first shot blew out the armoured windshield of the vehicle. His second shot dashed the automatic weapon from his attacker's hands. His third destroyed the door and flying particles wounded the other gunman. With his fourth he blasted the engine into junk.

The attackers fled, staggering dizzily. He hurried them on their way with well-placed explosions at their heels until they dropped into a gulley and vanished from sight.

"A complaint will be filed," he muttered, dusting himself off. "The Galactic Census up with this treatment will not put."

He examined the tracked vehicle and regretted that he had put it out of commission so completely. The buildings at the end of the field were a long hot distance away. While he was considering his next step another dust cloud appeared in the distance and this time he took the precaution of staying behind the wrecked vehicle until he found out what further mischief was in store.

The latest arrival, in a four-wheeled car, approached at a much slower pace and braked to a stop at extreme gunshot range.

"I'm all alone!" the driver shouted. "And I'm unarmed." He waved his hands in the air to prove the point.

"Drive forward slowly," the Commander answered, framing the figure in his sights.

The man really was alone and he climbed down, shaking with fear or apprehension, his fingers twitching towards the sky. "I'm the sheriff," he said, "and I'd like to talk to you."

"Talking is fine, shooting is not," Commander Sergejev said, coming into sight, his hand resting on his holstered gun.

"Sorry about that, stranger, but some of the boys got kind of excited. Seeing a newcomer and all that. But I'm the sheriff and I sort of want to welcome you officially."

"That is more like it. I am Commander Sergejev of the Galactic Census and I am here to take the census of your planet."

"I don't know if we have a census, I've never heard of one around here . . ."

"If we could go to your office, which is hopefully air-conditioned, I would be glad to explain," the Commander said, trying to keep the disgust from his voice. The stupidity of some of these backward planets was beyond belief.

"Now that's what I call a good idea. If you'll get in I'll take you right there now."

It was a brief ride, the car apparently had only one speed—full ahead—and they slid to a stop in front of the row of decaying buildings. The sheriff led the way down a littered hall to an office and the Commander followed him in.

As he came through the door a man stepped out and grabbed him about the body, pinning his arms.

Roaring with anger the Commander stamped hard on the man's instep, broke the hold and reached for his gun. But the others were on him by that time—men who had been concealed in the next room, in the closet, and one who had even been hiding under the desk. They overwhelmed him and bore him to the floor despite his bellows and struggling. His gun was whisked away and he was tied neatly with swift bights of rope.

"What is the meaning of this?" he shouted. "Do you know what you are doing . . ."

"We know right enough," the sheriff said, with an evil glint to his eye. "Our last plant manager died and the machines can't look after themselves for ever. We got a good job for you."

6

"AND that is my story, all of it," Sergejev shouted, and paced back and forth, his chain rattling and clanking behind him. "I have been here ever since. A victim of these aboriginal cretins. I have slaved for them and lived with the reality of this system, of free enterprise run wild, the ultimate extreme of laissez faire. The people here are incredibly selfish, completely untrusting, and fantastically lazy. They herd their beasts and feud with each other—and that is the whole of their lives. The Forbrugeners built this completely automated and self-repairing packing planet—and the locals are too lazy even to watch it themselves. Instead they capture me, a complete stranger, and imprison me here to keep an eye on the machinery."

"You didn't refuse?"

"Of course I refused!" Sergejev roared. "So they didn't bring me any food. Now I co-operate. It is an idiot's job in any case, merely watching the dials. The machines do everything, everything. Now you will release me and we will leave this place for ever."

"Soon, soon," Henry said, and the computer matched his soothing voice with a warm grin on the robot. "You're in no danger here and as soon as my investigation is complete we will leave . . ."

"Now! Now!" Sergejev thundered.

"You must understand that I have a responsibility to the people here as well as to you. And you are just making yourself more angry by choking this robot; it accomplishes nothing. The first O in R.O.B.O.T. stands for *obtrusion*—and that is what we do. We poke our noses in where we are not wanted. There is something very wrong with this planet and I intend to find out what it is. You will be safe where you are until my mission is accomplished. It should not take more than a few days . . ."

"You leave me here alone. You *sveenya, sabahkah, gloopwy* . . ."

"My, what a fine command of your native tongue you still have after all your years of travel! You won't be lonely, since this robot will stay hooked through to my computer. It can sing you songs, read books. You'll have a jolly time until I check back."

Henry quickly cut the circuit, since Commander

Sergejev was still bellowing, and a number of the words were familiar now.

"Three vehicles are approaching the ship," the computer announced.

"Seal the tunnel leading to the counter, load the counter back aboard the ship and lock the hatch. The water cooler and other odd items are expendable."

"It shall be done as you say."

Henry left the buried ship and trod a slow and thoughtful course back to his own ship. His brow furrowed in concentration, so he neither saw the chill beauty of the snowy mural nor heard the melodic rhythms of the background music. The tunnel that had formerly terminated under the counter had been filled in, and a welding robot was sealing a plate over the entrance when he passed. A one-man elevator was waiting where the tunnel terminated and, as soon as he stepped into it, it moved smoothly up through the ground and the hollow landing leg, up into the ship.

Henry dropped into his chair before the console in the control room and threw a switch. The screen flickered to life and he had a fine picture from a pickup high on the hull. The arm was just loading the last of the goods into the ship and the lock was closing. At the same moment the three tracked vehicles were sliding to a stop on the sand below; one of them neatly demolishing his water cooler. Men jumped out and there were flashes of light as they fired up at the ship. Somewhere, on the hull below, he could hear the ping of projectile against metal hull. They would have to mount heavier weapons than this if they were to make any impression on the ship. Some of the men put their heads together to confer, then boarded their vehicles again and rushed away.

"Always in a hurry," Henry said. "Gone away to think up more mischief, I suppose." He brooded. "And I have been thinking too. There is something very wrong with this planet."

The ship, since no question had been put to it, did not answer, but listened quietly, its patient breath the whispered exhalation of the air purifier. Henry looked glumly through the ports at the sun setting over the dusty plain.

"I'm hungry," he said. "Give me food for my thoughts. Steak, some of the Slagter beef we picked up on Forbrugen. It should be aged well after its multi-million-mile round trip."

"Medium rare, green salad with garlic dressing, garlic bread, and a bottle of the best red wine."

"All fine, except nix the garlic. It will spoil my public image if I have to talk to anyone—and will give me away in the dark if you want a more practical reason."

The sun slipped behind the horizon before a showy backdrop of purples, red-golds and greens as dinner arrived. Henry ate and drank well, and the weight of good food in his stomach drew deep thoughts from his brain.

"Though our friend, the good Commander Sergejev, has been over a year on this planet, I still think that his observations are wrong. This place is far more complex than he thinks it is. Do your voluminous records contain any indication of his past history?"

"They do. Before transferring to the Galactic Census he

was in Patrol, a cruiser commander, invalided out with wounds, and over age."

"Fine! A rough tough soldier with little interest in sociology, anthropology, exobiology or any other of the fine ologies that make the wheels go round. We shall ignore the Commander's observations and make some of our own. There are factors to this society that are very puzzling. Just think about them. Why do the children avoid the adults so continuously and well? Not children— just boys. Not girls, and there have been no women in sight. Why? And why all the individual locks on the slaughterhouse door?"

"I do not have enough material in my records to answer any of those questions."

"Then we'll get some more facts. Let's look at one of their homes first. I assume that you have been recording all the information from the robot that Silas Enderby purchased as a bodyguard?"

"I have."

"Show me his master's home, inside and out."

The picture on the screen flowed evenly towards them as they approached a building with a blank front. Not completely blank. Although it had no windows it was pierced by narrow openings not unlike gun slits. Perhaps they were. The robot followed his purchaser around behind the building where a deep-set entrance was protected by a thick wall. Silas leaned close to an opening beside a steel-bound and riveted door.

"Sound," Henry ordered.

"The stream it flows," Silas said.

"The grass it grows," another voice answered from the opening and the door ground slowly open.

"Password and countersign," Henry said. "That's more like a fortress than a home."

It was. There was an arms rack inside the door that held automatic weapons and drums of ammunition, as well as a grenade dispenser. In a guided tour of the house Henry saw the controls for a complex burglar alarm and detection system, reserves of food, water and compressed oxygen, in case the building were sealed against gas attack, as well as a portable generator for emergency power. Even more interesting was the tantalizing glimpse of a woman and two young girls seen through a rapidly closing door. They seemed to keep themselves apart from the main section of the house, and the master of the establishment did not enter their sector.

"Stranger and stranger," Henry mused. "It is time to do a little first-hand investigating. Do you think you can get me inside that fortress-cum-dwelling without raising the alarm?"

"A simple task. The robot can easily handle the alarm systems."

"Then let's move. Roll out a unicycle and fly cover with the spy-eyes."

"You will want a combat robot for protection?"

"I will not. Those things are as quiet as a collapsing landing leg. I'll count upon my speed and your intelligence network to keep me out of trouble." He rose, clamped his derby on his head, and left.

There was a concealed exit from the hollow landing leg that was less obvious than opening one of the hatches. The unicycle was waiting, standing upright and humming expectantly. This was a one-wheeled, or rather one-globed, vehicle that was held balanced upright by an internal gyroscope. The sphere on which it moved was soft, resilient and silent, and made only the slightest whisper of sound as he moved off into the darkness. Before and behind him the spy-eyes flew invisible guard.

"What's the news from town?" Henry asked.

"As of this moment six of the bugs have been destroyed by accident; none of them has been detected. Forty-three different individuals are now under constant observation. There is a large ditch ahead, I suggest you veer slightly to the right."

"Give me a guide then, it's a dark night. Shortest and best route to town. What is the Sheriff doing?"

A dim green light appeared in the air ahead of him as one of the spy-eyes swooped low to guide him. He followed it. The computer spoke again, through the tiny receiver pressed to the bone behind his ear.

"He is now eating dinner with a woman he refers to as 'wife'. There is something strange about this meal."

"Exotic eating habits? If it's too awful don't tell me."

"I do not mean that, but in the manner in which the meal is served. All the dishes are in covered pots. The Sheriff first served wife from each of them, then sat, uneating as she ate. When she had tasted each dish in turn she passed the plate to him and he is now finishing it."

"Nothing strange about that at all. Flip through your index and look up food-tasters, Old Earth."

"I see what you mean," the computer answered, after the briefest of intervals. "He is afraid of being poisoned, so eats only food that someone else has tasted without suffering ill effects. Please slow your vehicle and be prepared to turn left. I shall guide you through the quietest streets to the place you seek—STOP."

The unicycle skidded and shuddered to a stop, its gyro whining to hold it upright, as Henry hit the brakes.

"Would you mind telling me why?" he whispered.

"There are three people waiting around the corner of that building. They are obviously in hiding and are observing the ship. There is one woman and two children. One of them is the boy referred to as Robbie whom you conversed with earlier today. The other is a girl of approximately the same age."

"Any guns in sight? I remember the boy was looking for one."

"No weapons are detectable."

"All right. Hook me through to a speaker in a spy-eye and bring it close to them."

"Ready. It is hovering over their heads."

"Hi down there. This is Henry Venn speaking. Did you want to see me?"

Muffled shrieks and a grunt of surprise echoed in Henry's receiver, then a woman's voice spoke. "Where are you—I can't see you?"

"Close by, speaking by radio. Did you want to see me?"

"Yes, please, it is very important." Even through the radio linkage he could detect the strain in her voice.

"I'll be right with you."

They were waiting, huddled in the shadows, with the boy standing protectively in front.

"This is not my idea," he said, stepping forward, his

fists clenched. "I'm not even sure I like it. But my mother said she was going to go anyway, so I had to come. Keep an eye on her, you know."

"I do indeed. And very right too. I'm very pleased to meet you, madam," Henry said, tipping his hat in his most courtly manner.

"You must help me. When you leave this planet you must take my son and daughter to Forbrugen with you. They'll be expected there."

"I won't go," the boy said firmly. "But Kitt can go, that's all right."

Slagter's inner moon had risen and it cast a faint light into the shadows below the wall. Kitt was a teenager like her brother, a year or two older perhaps, nearer fifteen. She looked very much like her mother, a handsome woman with pale skin and long, dark hair.

"What do you say about all this, Kitt?" Henry asked.

"It's so far away, I know I shall never come back. I don't want to leave Mother but . . . at the same time . . . I know she's right." The girl was close to tears.

"Of course I'm right, you know that, you have eyes," her mother said. She stepped close and looked up at Henry. "You're an offworlder, so I can talk to you. You'll never believe what it means to be a woman on this planet. It's not hard—but it's like being in prison. My daughter can escape this. I've been secretly in touch with the authorities on Forbrugen. They assure me that this planet has a credit reserve there that they will apply to educational scholarships for any Slagter children. They are very much in favour of the idea. Will you do it?" There was naked appeal in her eyes.

"It might be arranged, though I am not leaving at once. And there are complications . . ."

"Take cover!" a spy-eye warned, swooping low. "Vehicles approaching, gunfire."

7

THEY dived for shelter, Henry pulling his unicycle after him, as the first crackle of shots was heard. Crouched low, Henry watched the two half-tracks roar towards them out of the night. Headlights flared and bobbed and the engines roared. The drivers were apparently driving with one hand and shooting with the other—which helped neither their driving nor their accuracy. Bullets splatted and whined as the vehicles rushed by and vanished around a bend. The popping and banging died away into the distance.

Henry rose and looked around, and discovered that he was alone. A spy-eye dived close. "They have returned home," it said. "I can lead you to the building if you wish."

"Not now. We have some more pressing business first. I'm going to interview a Slagteran on his home ground and get some answers to my questions. Blink your little tail light at me and lead on."

The spy-eye swooped away while Henry started up his unicycle and followed it.

"The next building on the right," the computer whispered into his ear.

"I recognize it. Now what's the drill?"

"The robot has disconnected the alarms on the front door and has placed a radio-operated relay in the door-opening circuit. When you reach the door I will open it."

"Watch the bike," Henry said, standing it in a dark corner and switching off the motor. "I have no idea how long this will take."

He approached the door, which opened silently as he came near. He stepped through quickly as the thick metal door swung back again, threatening to catch him as it closed. His surroundings were drab and confining—a narrow hallway, scarcely wider than his shoulders, that was illuminated by a dim bulb in a metal cage. He had to scuttle sideways to get past the rack of weapons and ammunition beside the door. Very efficient. More fortress than home. But why? Henry had the feeling that if he could answer this question he would be able to answer even more questions about this puzzling planet.

The main hallway inside seemed normal enough by anyone's standards—if you ignored the occasional locked case of gas grenades, the quaintly displayed trench knives and spiked clubs. But there was a hooked rug on the floor, a patch of outstanding colour in the overall drabness, and a few framed pictures on the wall. Henry was looking at one of these, a tropical island in a blue sea, that had been clipped from a magazine, when the bodyguard robot slipped through a door at the far end of the hall, closing it silently behind itself.

"Report," Henry said.

"Silas Enderby is finishing his dinner, Mrs. Enderby is

serving him, while the young Enderbys watch a taped space opera on the video."

"Fine. Take me to your master."

The robot nodded, opened the door and stepped aside so Henry could enter. He did so, raising his hat as he came, smiling broadly and greeting them in his friendliest manner.

"Sir and madam, good evening to you both and I sincerely hope that you have dined well."

Mrs. Enderby squealed shrilly, a sound somewhere between that of a stepped-on cat and a kicked pig, dropped the serving dish that she was holding and rushed sobbing from the room with her apron over her face. Her husband responded no less enthusiastically. He sat frozen, bulge-eyed, a spoonful of dessert half raised to his mouth, making little choking noises. As Henry came forward he shook off the paralysis with frenzied effort and clawed his revolver from its holster. But the hammer mechanism became entangled in the tablecloth and swept most of the dishes to the floor as he struggled. Henry, shaking his head remorsefully, reached over and freed the weapon and took it from the man's unresisting hand.

"How . . ." Silas gasped, "How . . . you get in here . . . ?"

"Simple," Henry said, and quickly prepared a white lie. "I knocked on the door and your faithful bodyguard robot let me in."

"Traitor!" Silas mumbled through tight-clamped teeth. He produced another, smaller pistol and fired two shots at the robot before Henry also relieved him of this weapon. The bullets ricocheted off the robot's steel abdomen and buried themselves in the wall.

"No one," Silas mumbled, "No one ever in this house. No one . . ." He sat, glassy-eyed, staring into space.

"I would not doubt that for a second," Henry said, rooting through his jacket pockets. "Now, I was brought up in a friendlier place and by my standards your degree of hospitality leaves a certain amount to be desired. But I'm not complaining, mind you. Live and let live, that's my motto. I've seen a lot of worlds and some of them more pugnacious than yours, though that takes a lot of doing. No insult intended, of course." He finally located his sales book and spread it on the table before them. "If I could have your signature here on the bill of sale, Mr. Enderby, I won't be bothering you any more. Sale isn't legal without it and I know we both want a legal sale, yes sir."

Still in a state of shock, Silas scribbled his name on the form—then shrank down in the chair.

"Kill me," he whispered hoarsely. "I know you came to kill me. Get it over with, quick, so I don't feel the pain."

"Nothing of the sort, Silas old customer," Henry said, and clapped the shivering man on the shoulder. Silas moaned and almost passed out. "That's not my way. I look for customers, not corpses. You are no good to me at all, sir, if you are dead."

"You're not killing me?" Silas asked in wonderment, sitting up straighter in his chair.

"Farthest thing from my mind. I'll sell you another robot if you want one, though."

"Traitor!" Silas shouted, glaring at the silent robot.

"Just doing his duty," Henry said, pulling up a chair and sitting down. "Don't worry about that robot. He'll guard you as long as there is a drop of oil left in his body. It's a machine, don't forget that, programmed to be always on your side. Not like people, many of whom can't be trusted."

"Don't trust anyone." Silas moved his chair away from Henry's at the thought and looked longingly at an axe-pickaxe combination mounted on the wall.

"I can believe that," Henry answered, apparently flipping through his order book but keeping a close eye on the twitchy Silas at the same time. "I wonder why that is?"

"They want to kill me," Silas said, looking everywhere except at his hand which was moving slowly down the sideboard towards a fruitbowl filled with handgrenades.

"Undoubtedly. And they want to kill me and each other just as strongly. What interests me is the reason *why*? What causes this universal suspicion and hatred? There must be a reason for it."

"Die, assassin!" Silas shouted and dived for the grenades. As he grabbed one up Henry jerked his thumb towards the robot.

"Very dangerous, master," the robot said as it reached down and plucked the grenade from the man's clasped fingers. He put it back with the others and moved them all out of reach. "I protect your life, sir. If that grenade had gone off in this small room you would have been sure to suffer injury."

Silas shivered away from the robot and began to chew his nails desperately. Henry pretended to ignore the entire incident.

"I wonder why that is, why everyone is so on the

defensive on this planet? What happened to start this? What are you afraid of?"

"The Wild Ones. They want to get us. The Wild Ones. Out there. Waiting."

"The Wild Ones?" Henry's ears almost drew themselves into points at this unexpected bit of information. Was this the missing explanation? "Who are they?"

"Wild Ones, out there in the hills. Hiding, raiding our herds, kill anyone they can. They are the ones." Silas bobbed his head rapidly at the seriousness of the thought. Henry picked up his enthusiasm.

"The Wild Ones. They sound pretty wild. They must be, to cause all this trouble. Well, I have to go now, Silas. Thanks for the hospitality. No need to see me out, I know the way."

But Silas was already on his feet, restored to jittery life at the thought that the intruder was now really going. He followed a pace behind Henry all the way down the hall and took a quick look around with an armoured periscope before he let him open the door.

"Quickly now, out, and don't come back!"

"It's been nice seeing you too," Henry said, jumping to stay ahead of the swiftly closing door. He stepped into the street and at the same moment the world exploded into noise and sound. He rocked back, deafened, looking for shelter where there was none. With a great roar the wall of the building just across the street blew outwards in a tumbling shower of debris and a half-track roared out of the ruin straight towards Henry: its headlights pinned him like a bug against the wall. Guns were firing on all sides now and bullets splatted into the wall above his head.

8

FIRST one, then the other headlight went out, and the half-track careered out of control. Henry leaped back as it crashed into the wall close to him.

The shooting continued. More vehicles were charging in now and gunfire rolled like thunder. An answering fire began from the house and something exploded in the roadway with a great booming, sending out a gout of flame. The door was closed again—and undoubtedly locked—so Henry dived for his unicycle and jumped into the saddle.

But he had turned it off, and the gyro had stopped. It started forward slowly, emitting a horrible rattling moan, weaving and tilting like a bucking broncho. Henry fought for control and managed to wobble erratically into the street and point the thing away from the fair-sized battle that was raging behind him. As the motors picked up speed the unicycle straightened up and began to roll faster.

"Fast is still not fast enough," he shouted, holding his hat down so that it wouldn't blow away. "And, ever-watchful robot-of-a-thousand eyes, would you mind telling me what all this is about? Sort of took us by surprise, didn't it?"

"I'm very sorry, but it is impossible to know every-thing . . ."

"You always talk like you do!"

". . . or to examine every building. It appears now that person or persons unknown were concealed in that building. They had the one you entered under observation. Their plan was obviously to force entrance when next the door was opened. It appears that, just by chance, you became involved."

"Did they break in?"

"No. I crashed a spy-eye into each headlight and the attack missed the door in the darkness. There are other vehicles involved, and I regret to say that one of them is now following you."

"I was wondering when you would notice that," Henry growled, turning the power full on, chasing his own shadow that was thrown by powerful headlights behind him. "Can you knock his lights out?"

"I have only two spy-eyes in the vicinity and I need one to keep contact." A headlight vanished as the words vibrated in Henry's head. "But the other was expendable. Might I suggest a turn as soon as possible, since there is another vehicle approaching ahead to cut you off. I am monitoring their radio contact."

"Jam it!"

"I have already done that, but the other party knows your location and direction."

Headlights flared ahead, rushing towards him.

"I would suggest the next right turning," the computer said. Henry twisted the handlebars. "No! Not this one . . ."

The wall loomed up ahead, his brakes squealed, he jumped free and rolled as the unicycle slammed into the solid bricks. He came out of the roll, dizzy, bruised, right up against the wall, with the computer's last words ringing in his skull.

". . . not this one. It's a dead-end alley. The next turning."

"You're just a little late with that information," he gritted between his aching teeth as he dragged himself painfully to his feet, pushing up against the brim of his hat which had been jammed down over his eyes. "Do you have any brilliant suggestions as to how I am to get out of this predicament?" He looked on gloomily as a half-track slid to a stop, blocking the alley mouth, and two men jumped down and ran towards him.

"You are leaving," the spy-eye whispered in his ear just as something exploded with a dull thud and the alley filled with impenetrable smoke. "If you will follow me."

"I would like to—if I could see," Henry said, and coughed as he breathed in a lungful of the light-absorbing smoke. Something nudged his shoulder.

"Touch the spy-eye," the computer said.

Henry let his fingers rest lightly on the humming tailplane of the hovering spy-eye and followed, stumbling, down the alley. He heard footsteps shuffle by him, followed by a metallic crash as someone fell over the ruin of his unicycle. Loud explosions echoed and bullets ricocheted and whined away invisibly. Something metallic brushed Henry's face and he lashed out.

"That is a ladder," the computer said.

"*Now* you tell me."

"If you will climb on to it you will be lifted out of here by the skyhook which is hovering above you. I presume you wish to return to the ship?"

"You presume wrong," Henry said, feeling for the ladder with his feet and planting them solidly on a rung.

"Up, up and away. Let's head for the hills. I want to meet one of those Wild Ones that Silas was talking about."

The ladder shivered under his weight, then moved upward with easy power. A moment later he was above the roiling smoke cloud, from which there still sounded the sharp crackling of gunfire. The separate, fortlike buildings of the city were spread out below him and the dark mass of the mountains loomed in the distance. The black disc of the skyhook, a heavy-duty cargo-lifter, blotted out the stars above him. A spiderlike robot clambered down the ladder and rested one claw on his shoulder as it leaned forward to speak into his ear.

"Little can be done at night. I suggest we return to the ship and in the morning . . ."

"Silence, you maternalistic mother-hen of a dim-witted computer. I say to the hills and to the hills we go. Get me a sleeping bag or something and I shall sleep rough under these alien stars. And while I'm asleep you can flit your little spy-eyes about and do an infrared survey of the hills and find some of these Wild Ones for me to take a look at in the morning. Understood?"

There was a moment's hesitation before the answer came, which indicated either computer cognition or robotic petulance.

"It shall be as you say. Do you intend to travel on this ladder?"

"I do. The night is cool after that scorcher of a day and I find the breeze refreshing after our little motor accident. Carry on."

The dark landscape rushed by silently and the foothills began to rise from the featureless grass plains. The hills had a mixed covering of forest and meadow with the occasional glint of starlight on water. As they came close to the sheer cliffs of the mountain range the skyhook slowed to a stop, then began to descend. There was a grassy bowl below set against the rock wall, with cliffs falling away on the front and sides.

"This spot is inaccessible," the spider said, "and invisible from the foothills below. I hope you will be comfortable here."

"So do I," Henry said, yawning, "since I suddenly feel the need of sleep."

Diffused lights sprang up as Henry descended and he saw that the ship had been busy. He had asked for a sleeping bag "or something" and the computer had made the most of the vagueness of this last remark. A pyramidal tent was staked out on the grass, gay with bunting and colourful flags. Lights glowed within it, striking golden glints from the brass bedstead with its turned-back crisp linen. Under the canopy before the tent a table had been set and an easy chair drawn up next to it. As Henry's feet touched the ground tiny flames snapped out from the hovering spy-eye to light the candles. They shone enticingly on a dish of caviare, thin sliced toast, finely chopped raw onion and hardboiled egg. The spider robot sprang from Henry's shoulder and raced over to the wine bucket, swarming up it to clasp the bottle of chilled champagne by the neck.

"A small snack before retiring," it said, sinking steel claws into the cork. "Always most restful." There was a sudden pop, the cork flew and champagne bubbled.

Henry dropped into the chair and took the glass.

"Very kind of you," he said, sipping. "Your empathy and psychological counselling circuits must really be working overtime tonight." He took a caviare-coated piece of toast from the robot and nibbled on it. "Not that I can find fault. I always did enjoy rugged camping in the wilderness."

Henry stumbled to bed and fell into such a deep sleep that the wash robot had to play brass band music at double amplification at dawn to rouse him.

"Away," Henry muttered, waving his hands fitfully with his eyes still closed. "Away with the kettle drums at this hour." The music changed abruptly to a string quartet as he swung his feet to the ground, shivering at the cold touch. "Report."

The wash robot snapped a basin down from its chest and filled it with warm water from a spigot at the end of one finger. "I found a number of heat sources during the night and at first light eliminated the large animals as not possibly being the Wild Ones. They are all herbivores of a shy and retiring nature, depending upon flight and fleetness of foot for survival. However, there are at least five aboriginal human beings in the immediate vicinity who are heavily armed with crude weapons and appear to fit the description of the Wild Ones as given."

"Humanoid natives of this planet?" Henry asked, wetting his face and accepting a squirt of liquid soap in his palms from the robot's little finger.

"Highly unlikely. Under photometric comparison they appear human to seven decimal places. We may safely theorize that they are human beings now living in this crude fashion for reason or reasons unknown." The robot extruded a comb into Henry's hand and its faceplate silvered and became a mirror. As Henry combed his hair the robot produced a pre-dentifriced toothbrush and began industriously to brush his teeth.

"More and more interesting," Henry mumbled around the brush. "We'll take a closer look at one of these throwbacks right after breakfast."

A cup of steaming black coffee was slipped into his hand and, feeling slightly more human, he sipped at it and went out to the table. He dined well on grilled sausage and fried cornmeal mush, then took his coffee with him while he strolled to the cliff edge to enjoy the impressive view as the foothills emerged from the morning fog. Behind him robotic feet rushed as all the equipment was stowed in crates and whisked skyward by the cargo lifter.

"I am ready," Henry said, pressing the *dispose* button on the cup and throwing it over the cliff. It disintegrated into a cloud of fine dust before it had dropped ten feet. "How do we contact our subject?"

"The skyhook will take you as close as possible without your being observed," the robot spider said, riding the ladder that swung close to Henry: he grabbed a rung. "I will guide you the rest of the way."

9

IT was a brief ride, with the ladder pulled up just under the belly of the skyhook so that they could stay below the ridge lines as they followed a branching valley back towards the plains.

"We have arrived," the spider said as they hovered over a grassy bank. It jumped to the ground and Henry followed. "Just over this ridge and I recommend great quietness in walking."

"I recommend shutting up. Just lead the way and let me worry about the sneaking-up part."

They proceeded in silence then, climbing through the knee-high grass and pushing under the lowhanging fronds of the trees. The spider silently led the way on to an outcropping of rock and pointed below. Henry took off his hat and laid it on the ground before crawling forward to look carefully over the edge. It was quite a sight.

What appeared to be a well charred and half eaten side of beef lay in a cold bed of ashes just below him. Next to it, half on the grass and half in the ashes, sprawled a singularly unattractive member of the human race. His clothes, if they could be called that, consisted of a collection of badly tanned furs laced together with rough strips of leather. Long knotted hair merged into an even longer and more tangled beard. Hair, furs and man were matted and filthy and now liberally strewn with ashes. The furs had fallen back to disclose the individual's monstrously engorged stomach that rose up like an overripe melon; he had obviously stuffed himself to partial extinction on the feast of burnt meat. Something troubled him now, undoubtedly his digestion, and he groaned and rolled without opening his eyes. His hand, which rested in the ashes, crawled over like an immense insect and plucked at the beef until it detached a fragment. This was conveyed to the gaping mouth and chewed and swallowed apparently without the feaster waking up.

"Very nice," Henry said, standing and brushing himself off and putting the derby back on his head. "There goes my appetite for the week. Let's see what Rosebud has to say for himself." The spider jumped to his shoulder as he slid down the slope to the dell below.

The Wild One was awake instantly, sitting up—which took quite an effort—and glaring at Henry from a pair of very piggy and bloodshot eyes.

"Very pleased to meet you, sir, and happy to see that you have dined well. Let me introduce myself . . ."

"Kill! Kill!" the Wild One grunted and took up the stone hammer that he had been lying on, hurling it at Henry in a single, surprisingly swift motion. Straight at his forehead. There was no time to dodge or to even raise his arm in defence.

The robot spider hurled itself from his shoulder, making eight nice little holes in his skin with its feet as it did so, and crashed into the hammer. Hammer and spider fell to the ground in a tangle of metal legs, the spider crushed and unmoving.

"I assure you, sir, that I mean you no harm . . ."

"Kill! Kill!" the Wild One mumbled again, feeling about for a fist-sized rock that he hurled as well. Prepared this time, Henry dodged the missile.

"Come now, we can discuss this like grown men . . ."

"Kill! Kill!" the Wild One screeched and rushed to the attack, fingers spread. Henry stepped inside the clawing arms and administered a swift chop with the side of his hand to the other's neck. Then stepped aside as the attacker went down and out.

"I am afraid that you and I have a problem in

communication," he said as he bent to wipe the greasy side of his hand on the grass. An insect buzzed about his head and he swatted at it before he heard the reedy voice it whispered with.

"Report. Another Wild One is coming this way up the ravine. He does not appear to be armed."

"A small blessing," Henry said, settling himself into a fighting stance, extended hands ready.

There was a rapid shuffle of approaching footsteps and the Wild One came into sight. He was as dirty as the other and wearing the same scruffy furs, but here the resemblance ended. For one thing he was much older, with grey hair and beard. Around his neck there was a fragment, so stained and soiled as to be unrecognizable, of what might have been a colourful neckcloth. Perched on his nose was the ruin of what had once been a pair of eyeglasses. One lens was gone and the other so chipped and cracked that it was almost translucent. The man stopped and put his head to one side when he saw Henry, blinking through the obscured glass, cackling lightly.

"Well, well well, what do we have here," he said, shuffling forward slowly.

"That's more like it," Henry said, lowering his guard. "It is a pleasure to meet you . . ."

"Pleasure, pleasure? Do not use that word loosely," the old man said, squatting next to the scorched side of beef. "Language is a precise instrument, words have values, words can do things. Like names. Take names. If I told you my name you would have a power over me, yes you would, names can do things." While he talked, in the calmest of voices, his fingers tore at the meat, unnoticed, and stuffed fragments into his mouth so that his words became muffled and unclear.

"I'm sure of that," Henry said, "and readily agree with you. But I must ask what an educated man like yourself is doing here, living in these conditions . . ."

"A holiday, nothing more." Munch, snap, his teeth tore at the meat. "Do not consider for a moment that I am from this backward planet, oh dear no. I am from Forbrugen, a man of science, here to observe the local life forms. Very interesting. I am writing a paper soon. A man of science and peace . . ."

"Mine! Mine!" the other Wild One said, stirring to life and rolling over to embrace the cooked carcass with both his arms. Still stuffing his mouth with one hand, the newcomer picked up a rock in the other and rapped the original owner of the feast smartly on the side of the head. With a single groan he collapsed back into the ashes. Henry watched silently but made no move to interrupt their fun.

"Very interesting," he said. "As a Forbrugener, an offworlder, you have a point of view that is most important. You perhaps know why the people on this planet are so suspicious and violent."

"I do." Chomp.

The silence lengthened until Henry finally asked, "Well—will you tell me?"

"Of course. Credit where credit is due, remember, and I publish first. It is all a matter of radiation, personal radiation, you know. There are evil emanations from evil thoughts, a radiation to which we can assign the value n.

When n is used in the equation with the locus of wave radiation l . . ."

There was more like this, much more, and Henry sighed loudly.

"Around the bend, poor chap," he told the little metal ornithopter that was now flapping in slow circles about his head.

"If you are referring to his sanity index you are correct," the ornithopter flapped back. "I have been running a comparison with known parameters in the records and find that, if on another planet, he would have a 97.89% chance of being confined in a mental hospital for corrective treatment."

"Make that 100%. A tragedy, an intelligent man who came here to study and who broke under the strain. We must see that he is sent back to Forbrugen."

"I have made a note for the records."

"Let's start back, there is nothing going for us here. These Wild Ones appear to be just that, loners and outcasts. They can't possibly be responsible for the difficulties on this planet . . . what's going on here?"

The old man looked up suddenly and put one hand to his ear. Then he tore a great chunk of meat from the carcass and rushed away with it. The other Wild One was not far behind. He groaned, sat up—then sprang to his feet and ran tottering out of sight.

"They have heard the approach of a party of track-cycles," the ship said. "They are coming this way from the direction of the herds on the plains."

"Now you tell me, always the last to know."

"There is no danger yet, I was waiting to inform you."

"Next time keep me informed from the beginning. How am I getting out of this?"

"A skyhook is on the way. I would suggest that you climb back to the rocks above until it arrives. The pursuers appear to be after the one who stole their animal, so they will undoubtedly continue the chase of the others."

"You better be right," Henry said, climbing as fast as he could.

It was a good vantage point. He could watch without being seen as the roaring track-cycles slid to a stop below.

"Here's the carcass!" one of the men shouted. "Rustled it, cooked and ate it. I told you we had a steer missing."

"Which way did he go?"

"The houndog will tell us."

Henry hissed at the ornithopter, which had folded its wings and landed next to his head. "What, if you don't mind my asking, is a houndog?"

The memory search of the computer took just microseconds.

"Hound dog, an animal much prized for its sense of smell and for its edibility, at different times and different places. Now the name is applied to a commercial tracking instrument that follows odour trails in the manner attributed to the original creature of that name."

"Where is the skyhook?" Henry asked, a sudden chill touching his spine.

"Just three minutes away—"

"Get it here!"

"Hey," a voice shouted from below. "Houndog found three trails. Two go off thataway and one leads straight up these rocks."

"Someone up there!"

"Let's get him!"

Henry did a good job, but he was just outnumbered. The track-cycles roared up the slope and were upon him. He pulled the first man from his saddle and sent him, unconscious, back against the others. Before the present assignment he had been a Patrol Marine and his carefully cultivated layers of fat covered some impressive musculature. And he knew how to fight. Three men were on the ground, moaning or unconscious, before the fourth got behind him with his pistol butt and completed the ruin of his derby hat. Henry never knew what hit him.

10

HENRY groaned, opened his eyes, did not like anything that he saw, groaned again and closed them.

"Explain what has happened!" Commander Sergejev said, bending over so close that his beard brushed Henry's nose.

"Away with the jungle," Henry answered, brushing feebly at the thing. "Tell me what you know while I make up my mind whether to live or die, and I'll fill in the rest of the details."

"Bah. You let yourself be captured. Now we shall rot in this automated slaughterhouse for ever."

"Patience. Try not to shout. I'll get you out of here—but just tell me what happened."

"You know what happened, or that robot that looks

like you knows what happened. I could not sleep, that creature never sleeps, so we were having a game of chess. When, suddenly, it leaps to its feet—on purpose spilling the pieces because I would have mate in four—and tears its leg chain loose from the wall. If I had known it could have done that, I would have forced it to release me long before this. Then it climbs to the top of the memory storage units and hides itself. While I am shouting at it, the door bursts open and they bring you in, looking like this. In a moment you are chained again, or for the first time, *Nyeboh*! you know what I mean, and they leave. And now your filthy robot ignores me completely, and is up there chopping a tiny hole in the wall. Madness!"

Henry looked up at himself, the robot self, hanging upside down by its legs just below the high ceiling, digging a hole in the wall with a length of steel. Dizzy, he closed his eyes again and groaned histrionically.

"I need a doctor," he said.

"Help is on the way," the robot called down, and poked the hole through. As soon as the hole was clear a spy-eye zoomed through and flashed down to the floor next to Henry. Its silver, birdlike shape hovered, humming expectantly, while a hatch slowly opened in its back. The robot dropped all the way back to the floor with a jarring thud and ran over. It pulled a package from the spy-eye— which swooped up and out of the opening again.

"A medical kit," the robot said. "I will now tend your wounds."

"Pain-killer first, you short-circuited excuse for a computer," Henry said. "And then an explanation."

The shot did its work instantly and, while the robot dressed his bruises and contusions, it explained.

"Stopping the men was out of the question since all I had were minor units in the vicinity. But I did succeed in preventing them from killing you, bugs in their weapons made them intolerable, and I ceased all operations as soon as you were unconscious and in their hands. I reasoned that you would be brought back here since this is where you were taken in the first place. I reasoned correctly."

"And if you had thought wrong . . .?"

"I was prepared for all eventualities," the computer answered with mechanical self-assurance. "By that time heavy units had been dispatched." Since some of the heavy units carried atomic weapons the self-assurance appeared justified.

Henry moved and sat up, and no longer had the feeling that he was going to fall to pieces when he did so.

"We leave here now!" Sergejev said, his fingers making twitching, throat-crushing motions.

"Yes, I guess so. We certainly can't accomplish very much chained in this butchershop control room. But— patience—give me a few moments to rally my vital forces."

"Ten minutes you have, no more!" Sergejev began to pace the room, glancing at his watch.

"You are the soul of generosity, Commander. How your men must have loved you."

"Perhaps they did, but they never told me. As long as they obeyed I was satisfied."

"You would never make a crewman out of anyone from this planet. I have never seen so many suspicious, single-minded people in all my life. The children seem normal enough, and the women, if you can call being in purdah normal. But the men! Treacherous, suspicious, murderous—pick your adjective. Perhaps the Forbrugeners were right when they said that the people here were just carried away by the frontier life and developed this kill and be-killed culture. They won't ship any powerful energy weapons here, and only a limited amount of explosive weapons. They have to send some or their prime source of protein would be cut off. It is a dilemma that appears not to have an easy solution. They are ingrained in their way of life here—and it is almost impossible to change all the mores of a society."

"Why change? Leave! Let them have their cows and dust and guns. They're mad, all of them, mad."

Henry's eyes widened and he sat suddenly bolt upright. "What did you say?"

"You heard what I said, mad. Now we go, time is up."

Henry swung his feet to the floor and slowly stood. "Maybe if they were all mentally ill it would explain a lot of things. I may have been looking for the wrong reasons . . ."

"No violence, if you please, Commander," the Henry-robot said, stepping between Henry and the angry census man, who was advancing with hands outstretched and fingers twitching.

"We're leaving, Commander, relax," Henry said, bringing his attention back to the affairs at hand. "Ship, I presume you can get us out of this building?"

"A simple affair," the robot answered, bending over

Henry's ankle chain. "If you would be so kind as to follow me, gentlemen."

With an easy snap it broke the chain off close to Henry's ankle, then did the same for Sergejev. They followed it to the door from the room—which it crashed through without slowing down. The two men stepped through the wreckage and followed the robot through the hallways to the outer door.

"It won't break that thing down as easily," Sergejev said, pointing at the thick, steel-reinforced beams of the door.

"If you will kindly step to one side," the robot said, pointing, and when they did so the entire door blew in, sending splinters and twisted bits of metal crashing into the far wall. They went out of the blasted opening to see a heavy-duty robot with an energy cannon mounted where its head should be. Its eyes and mouth were in its abdomen.

"I suggest a speedy withdrawal," it said. "Alarms have been triggered by your escape and it appears as if *all* the men in the city have been aroused and are on their way."

With this encouragement they ran, robots and men, through the thick darkness. Clouds covered the moon and stars, and the Slagterans did not believe in street lights. Warned by the ubiquitous bug and spy-eye robots they hid, turned aside, and sought cover to avoid the vehicles and men who were searching for them. When they finally reached the edge of the spaceport they saw the spaceship at the far end—surrounded by trucks and half-tracks. Searchlights and headlights lit up the surrounding area as light as day. Henry slid to a stop, panting heavily, and levelled an accusing finger at the nearest robot.

"Don't pretend you didn't know about this. Saving the news of this welcome party as a little surprise?"

"No. I did not inform you for the sake of your morale, judging that the news that the ship was surrounded might be depressing and interfere with your efficiency in flight."

"I'll impair your efficiency!" Sergejev shouted and kicked the robot in the ankle, which accomplished no more than to send shooting pains through his own foot.

"How do we get to the ship?" Henry asked.

"Follow me. The Commander's buried ship is almost outside the ring of guards, and I am angling a second tunnel up to ground level in a protected area. You may enter that way."

"We have no other choice. Let's go, Commander."

The lights were strong and they completed the last hundred yards crawling on their bellies through a shallow ditch. They were exhausted, filthy, and soaked with sweat, before they rolled into a gulley cut by the rain.

"We have arrived," the Henry-robot said. "If you will wait a few moments, please, the tunnel will hole through. In the meantime I would suggest absolute silence because units have detected an individual with a gun who is close by and coming in this direction."

"Can we capture him without raising the alarm?" Henry asked.

"That is possible. Please remain silently where you are."

They huddled against the dirt of the bank as heavy footsteps came close and a figure appeared above them, outlined against the glare around the ship. He had a revolver ready in one hand, and he shaded his eyes with the other as he tried to peer into the blackness below.

The Henry-robot reached up, with the slashing speed of a snake, and seized the searcher by both ankles. Before the man could cry out or raise his gun he was crashing down into the gulley next to them.

As he went by Henry hit him soundly on the point of the jaw. When he touched the ground he kept going, folding silently, unconscious. His face turned up towards the light from the sky and Henry cried out joyfully.

"Our old friend the Sheriff! I could ask for no better subject."

There was a rumble and grinding next to them and the shining metal of a whirling drill blade broke through the surface. An instant later the bulk of the drilling robot had crawled out of the raw hole in the ground and stood, vibrating, on its wide treads.

"Into the tunnel with haste," the Henry-robot advised. "I will drag the Sheriff after you. I must advise that this tunnel is not reinforced and has a duration expectancy of between three and four minutes before the roof collapses."

"You and your cheap tunnels!" Henry shouted, diving for the opening. Sergejev was right behind him. As soon as his feet had vanished from sight the Henry-robot crawled in, hauling the limp body of the Sheriff, with the drilling robot just behind him. In a moment they were gone and the combat robot remained alone, on guard.

11

IT was not much fun. The roof of the tunnel brushed Henry's back as he crawled on hands and knees. It was black and airless and he had been close to exhaustion when he started the mad crawl. There seemed to be no end to it and he felt the weight of all the dirt pressing down on him, collapsing on him, and he knew he would never make it.

And then the tunnel bent upwards and flattened out and he saw light ahead. He reached the opening into the reinforced tunnel with his last strength and collapsed in the opening. A waiting robot pulled him clear, then turned to extract the Commander like a cork from a bottle. The Henry-robot was next and it had pulled the Sheriff half-way out of the hole when the tunnel collapsed. The other two men could only sprawl, exhausted, while the robots dug him free.

"I thought that perhaps you would like a cold beer," another robot said, appearing out of the connecting tunnel. It carried a tray with two glasses and two frosted bottles of foaming beer. "Do you think the Commander would like to join you?"

The Commander growled something indistinguishable as he lurched out and grabbed one of the bottles. He scorned the glass and raised the bottle to his lips, and half drained it before he lowered it, gasping. Henry drank his in a slightly more leisurely manner.

"Your ship is right here, Commander," he said. "Buried but safe and sound. Would you care to join me in mine until we can get it unearthed?"

The escape and the beer had improved the Commander's mood considerably.

"I will be happy to join you. I have had enough of being underground for the moment, if you don't mind."

"I couldn't agree more."

They rose, groaning, and went down the tunnel to the ship. Before Henry cleaned up and put on a fresh coverall he turned the Sheriff over to the ship with precise instructions. He had his feet up, and was reading a computer printout report and eating a sandwich when Sergejev joined him.

"Sit down and order what you like, Commander," he said, waving towards a chair. "I'm glad to see the ship could find something your size to wear."

"Size yes, fabric no. Nothing except the same hideous check that you wear." He looked through a menu that a robot handed to him. "What is that very official-looking report you have there?"

"The answer to the Slagter problem. The Sheriff has a goodly quantity of DMPE, or taraxein as it is sometimes called, in his blood. Analysis has revealed its source."

The Commander indicated his choices, handed the menu back, and looked up at Henry, scowling, his old self again. "Are you mad?" he said.

"No, but the Sheriff is. Certifiably mentally ill, on any planet except this one. Do you know what paranoid schizophrenia is?"

"A form of mental illness. But what is the connection?"

"The Sheriff has it. The paranoid lives in his own world, knowing and trusting only himself. In one particular form of the disease the victim is subject to delusions of persecution. He believes that the whole world is against him. He may appear rational in all ways except this one. Just because a person is insane does not mean that he has to be stupid."

"Are you trying to tell me that . . ."

"Exactly. Every man on this planet is a certified hospital case. Paranoia was once thought to be of a strictly psychological order, stemming from childhood conflicts and such like. Eventually it was discovered that these events are only the trigger that sets off the illness, which is frankly chemical in origin. It is an abnormality of the brain chemistry. DMPE is an antibody, generated by the body mechanisms in response to foreign material. The trouble with DMPE is that it is injurious not only to the invading organism, but to the brain itself."

The Commander gaped. "Do you mean to tell me that this . . . DMPE, whatever you call it . . . is making the men mentally sick, so that they act the way they do? If so, where is the DMPE coming from?"

"The computer is still making microanalysis, but it has already found a microorganism that appears to be responsible. This is a single-celled and very weak bacterium that apparently invades the body tissues very slowly. But these forms of infection can be the worst kind, like leprosy, because their action is so slight that the body cannot rally its defences against the organism. So the microorganism persists, slowly getting stronger, while the body fights back, eventually producing enough DMPE to cause the secondary mental disease."

"How long?"

"It must be thirteen to fifteen years, because the children don't have the symptoms. But there is a boy here of about fifteen, who is obviously on the way."

"And the girls and women?"

"They must be naturally immune, that's the most

logical explanation, because the microorganism is every-where on this planet."

"Then we'll catch it!"

"Relax, of course we will. But it takes fifteen years to show any effects, remember. It will be licked in a matter of months now that we know what to look for. Medical teams will come here from Forbrugen and take things in hand."

Sergejev grabbed a sandwich which the robot brought in and took an immense bite, then waved the remainder at Henry. "That is the hole in your argument. If this disease is so widespread, then it must be in the meat, and how come it never spread to Forbrugen?"

"Simple enough. Long exposure at below freezing conditions will kill almost any organism after a matter of months. The meat is shipped from here frozen, and is months in space. There is no other contact with the surface of this planet."

"It makes sense," Sergejev grudgingly admitted, finishing the last crumbs of his sandwich and sending the robot out for a second. "In which case I must stay here after my ship is dug out. These people are sick, and they will be cured. And when they are cured I will count them for the Galactic Census and my job will be done."

"It will be a better life for all of them. The children can go away to schools on Forbrugen and when they return build a reasonable society here rather than this strange one." Henry smiled wryly. "That is surely an impressive thought."

"What?" Commander Sergejev asked, more interested in the sandwich and bottle of beer that was coming his way.

"The children. I imagine kids everywhere rebel when they're young, look down on the older generations, and even think that their parents are crazy for having the ideas they do.

"But here on Slagter—the kids are right!"

There was little more to be said. The ceremonies were brief. The Cadets stepped forward, heads high, and received their scrolls. One by one they repeated this simple ceremony until the last was done.

Cadets no more.

"Patrolmen, I greet you . . ." The Commanding Officer said, then his voice was drowned by the cheers of the happy men. Cheer after cheer echoed from the domed roof, dying away only as they rushed out to their assignments and their future, until only the Commanding Officer was left alone—already thinking of the new class that would be entering the next day.

Out they went from the hall, from Earth, to the planets and the stars of the galaxy, spreading law and order. Spreading it with the aid of faithful pigs, loyal robots, all the friends of mankind that have voyaged with him through space to aid in the conquest of the alien stars.

Hand in hand, pig, robot and man marched solidly into the wonderful future.